W9-AVC-662

R. H.

OUTCASTS OF REBEL CREEK

OUTCASTS OF REBEL CREEK

A Western Quartet

FRANK BONHAM
EDITED BY
BILL PRONZINI

SAGEBRUSH
Large Print Westerns

First published in Great Britain by ISIS Publishing
First published in the United States by Five Star

Published in Large Print 2007 by ISIS Publishing Ltd.,
7 Centremead, Osney Mead, Oxford OX2 0ES
United Kingdom
by arrangement with
Golden West Literary Agency

British Library Cataloguing in Publication Data
Bonham, Frank
    Outcasts of Rebel Creek: a western quartet. –
    Large print ed. – (Sagebrush western series)
    1. Western stories
    2. Large type books
    I. Title II. Pronzini, Bill
    813.5'4 [F]

ISBN 978–0–7531–7775–4 (hb)

Printed and bound in Great Britain by
T. J. International Ltd., Padstow, Cornwall

Table of Contents

BUTCHERKNIFE RIDGE

Well-realized characters and cleverly constructed plots utilizing unconventional elements were two of Frank Bonham's many strengths as a Western writer. "Butcherknife Ridge," which first appeared in *Five-Novels Magazine* (9-10/47), showcases both of these attributes. Ex-soldier and gambler Bill Devlin, one of the Devlin clan of "valiant drinkers and mighty brawlers" who for generations have raised hell in the Big Bend country of Texas, is typical of Bonham's tough but fair, rugged yet flawed protagonists — a man fighting to earn respect for himself while trying to clear the name of his grandfather, who was lynched for dynamiting a dam and drowning more than forty homesteaders in the ensuing flood. Politics, Mexican bandits, stolen money, family secrets, and a man's thumb floating in a bottle of mescal also figure prominently in this twist-laden action tale.

CHAPTER
ONE

OK

Johnson, the owner, had a room behind the saloon where he said Devlin could sleep. Devlin brought his bedroll inside, and they walked through the cool, dark saloon, the saloonkeeper collecting mugs from tables as he walked. He deposited them on the bar, and opened a door.

Bill Devlin went in. He stopped immediately to glance back at Bart Johnson. He stood with the bedroll balanced on his shoulder, a very tall, dark-skinned, young fellow. He sniffed the air, which held a faint memory of perfumed clothing.

"Bart," he said, "all I wanted was a room."

"That's a nice thing to say." Johnson, bluff and red-faced, liked to pretend that only the most respectable people patronized the Hub. "There was a lady staying here one day. A very nice young lady, in fact. She left yesterday."

"A very nice young commission lady?"

Johnson picked a blonde hairpin from the floor. "You know her. Old man Hunter's girl."

"Why, she's only . . ." Devlin hesitated. In his mind, she was only fifteen years old, and the town was still a dirty sprawl of mud buildings. But in the four years he'd been away, Chito had washed its face and grown a lot. No doubt the girls had grown a bit, too.

Johnson was nodding. "That's right, Bill. She was only . . . She ain't now. She's nineteen, and she kept right on growing. She made me put a bar on the door and used the back entrance."

"Why would she stay in a dump like this?"

Johnson opened the window for air. "Hotel's only half finished," he said. "She's been away, too. Just came back, and the ranch up the valley took some fixing before she could move in."

Devlin threw the roll of blankets on the cot. "I don't see why anybody'd come back, once he got away."

"Why did you come back?" Johnson challenged.

Devlin frowned. "See the old man, my grandfather, I guess, and make sure I was dead right in leaving here."

Johnson gave him a curious glance, and then looked away. "Well, stay as long as you want to, Bill," he said.

He went out, and Devlin lay down on the cot. His feet hung over the end, the middle sagged so that his hip pockets nearly touched the floor. It was the first time he had rested on anything like a bed in three weeks. In a few minutes he was asleep.

Saloonkeeper Johnson began dipping beer glasses in a dirty pail of water and standing them bottoms up on a towel spread on the bar. He took a melancholy pleasure in the thought that there was a Devlin sleeping in the back room again. They were all gone, the rest of the Devlins, those valiant drinkers and mighty brawlers, all but this one. A small, sunburned town lost in a small valley of the Big Bend of the Río Grande would never hold him. Whiskey, women, and belligerence had been the faults of the old ones. But for a final skyrocket flare at the end a drop of wanderlust had been added to the blood of Bill Devlin.

Bill Devlin awoke at sundown. A glass of whiskey had been placed on the chair beside him while he slept. He smiled. He sniffed it, grimaced, and set the glass down. In Chito, whiskey stank and burned.

From the window he could see the red, corrugated bluffs of the San Vicentes across the Big River. Redondo Valley, in which the town lay, was an irregularly shaped basin cut back and forth by the Río Grande. Within a half mile of the river on both sides were green, irrigated acres; up on the edges was the best pasture land in the Big Bend country, and behind that the land crumpled into rim rock and mountains.

Devlin could see a corner of the town and a wide area of farmed land. It was amazing the way Chito had grown. There were twenty or thirty new white-washed adobe homes, and a large section of land had been newly cultivated.

He took shaving apparatus from his bedroll. Through the door drifted a muffle of voices. They approached, Johnson's bass emerging. "Now listen, boys, he's asleep. He's tired, and, if he's like the rest of them, he won't be fit to talk to for an hour after he wakes up."

Someone drawled: "We'll take that chance."

The door opened quietly. Johnson looked relieved on seeing Devlin standing by the window, shaving. "How you feeling, Bill?"

"All right. Who's with you?"

Johnson came in with two other men. One was a very serious-looking man who wore a marshal's badge. The other, not over five feet tall, was a brown-skinned chunk of a man with black eyes in a broad, brown face. He had the shoulder breadth of a six-footer, but about a foot less height, just as though the man he had been had been logged over, like a tree, and he was the stump. But he was strong and deep-chested with alert eyes and only a little of the dwarf's spatulate deformity.

Bill put out his hand. "How's it going, Jarco?"

Jarco had been the town jester and carpenter. He had a new, serious manner now. He smiled briefly, and then glanced at his companion. "You don't know Marshal Cheney, I guess. Bill Devlin, Al."

Cheney solemnly shook Bill's hand. He was a strongly made young fellow with a taffy-colored beard framing his face. His mouth was a hard line that looked to Bill as though it wouldn't know how to smile if Cheney told it to. He was obviously a man who took himself very seriously.

"Bet you didn't know the old place, Devlin," he said.

Bill turned back to his shaving. "You've changed everything but the climate," he admitted.

"How do you like it?" Jarco asked, and he watched Devlin's face closely.

Devlin stropped the razor slowly across one of his chaps. Then he squinted at himself in the mirror as he placed the blade against a sideburn. He waited until he knew they thought he was not going to answer. He was aware that Cheney had come here, not with a welcome, but with the stock warning for a Devlin in town: *No rough stuff, mister!*

Cheney cleared his throat.

"Why, it looks all right," Bill remarked.

"Everything's changed!" Jarco declared. "Lots of people coming in. We're clearing more land every year. Even got a school!"

He gestured largely with a hand that lacked a thumb. He had had a full quota of thumbs when Bill left, and Bill assumed he was still at his old trade of carpentry.

Devlin slapped a blob of lather on the floor. "I got out just in time, didn't I?"

Cheney sat on the cot. Devlin's Frontier model Colt in its black holster lay on the floor near his feet. In the mirror, Devlin's eyes watched him. He thought: *Somebody told this guy he looked like Wyatt Earp, and he's trying to live up to it. Two guns! And of all the fool beards!*

"What are your plans?" Cheney asked. It was an innocuous question, but it was put in the hearty, over-friendly manner of a man handling a dangerous drunk.

Devlin's shoulders stirred. "Oh . . . get drunk, I guess. Raise hell. That what you mean?"

The marshal started. Then his light blue eyes toughened. "I know you're joshing, Devlin, but it's not the kind of joshing I like. I like to say hello to everybody that comes in town, but there's another way I can put it. Make trouble for me, and I'll make trouble for you. Is that the way you like it?"

Devlin looked at Johnson. "Where's this guy's sense of humor? They usually laugh like hell when I say that."

Jarco grinned. "He's just kidding, Al. Well, we'll see you around, Bill. Just make yourself at home."

Bill said soberly: "Thanks."

He halted in the act of turning back to the mirror. His arm swung and from the blade of the razor a puff of wet lather slipped, to sail silently across the room and strike Marshal Cheney on the side of the head. Cheney's hand had been about to pick up Devlin's gun. It jerked away, and he touched the lather on his face.

"If you want to look at a man's gun," Devlin said, "ask him. Don't wait until he turns his back and then reach for it."

Cheney's face reddened. "You'd better get hold of that temper," he said flatly. "I was just going to take the number for your permit."

"For my what?"

"Your permit to carry a gun. It's an ordinance. If a man gets in too many scrapes, he loses it. If he's caught wearing a gun without a permit, he goes to jail. If you want to carry that thing, come around to my office and I'll fill out your permit."

He wiped the soap on the bed and went out. Jarco followed.

Devlin stared at the saloonkeeper. "Am I crazy?"

Johnson shook his head. He stepped out to the bar and brought a bottle back. Seeing the full glass on the chair, he asked: "How am I going to fill that if you don't empty it?"

Devlin began to whip up lather in the mug. "Got any J. H. Cutter?"

Johnson revolved the bottle. "I get all my stuff across the river. Save tax."

"Thanks just the same then, Bart."

The saloon man sat down. "You mean you're refusing a drink?"

Devlin grinned at him in the mirror. "First time it's ever happened, eh?"

Johnson drank the whiskey himself. He shook his head. "You're no son of Johnny Devlin, nor grandson of Harry. Why, the way I've been hearing it, you've had yourself quite a time. Got in a revolution in Mexico, didn't you? Killed two men in Eagle Pass and spent six months drunk in San Angelo."

Devlin laughed, his humor not reaching very deep. It was funny, if you hadn't been exposed to it all your life. He supposed the revolution Johnson spoke of was the year he had spent hiring for a railroad on the Isthmus. He had been in a few scraps, and any one of them might have been expanded into a multiple killing.

"I'm a pretty rough boy, all right, Bart," he said. "I play my cards close to my chest and I never sit with my back to a door. But I sure can't drink that whiskey of yours."

Johnson placed the bottle on the table. "I'm going to put this right here, anyway, because you'll need it. Bill, that was the mayor you were just talking to. The small, dark gentleman!"

"Jarco?"

"Jarco. Remember when he used to do odd jobs around town? He'd do carpentry for me when the boys broke up the chairs. Now he tells me where to bury my garbage and taxes me for selling whiskey. I guess he's all right, a smart little galoot, but put any guy like him in a job like that and he'll throw his weight around."

Devlin began to wipe scraps of lather off his face. "Why did you elect a mayor in the first place?"

"It was Charlie Amory's idea. Remember Charlie? The good state of Texas sent him to the U.S. Senate after he'd served so nobly in the state legislature. Well, he got sick after a year and came home. But I guess he'd been in Washington too long, at that. He stumped around the state getting settlers to come in. About thirty families that had never seen the Bend fell for it. Amory built a school and laid out a new irrigation system after he rebuilt the dam."

"What do you mean . . . rebuilt it?"

Johnson scratched his neck. "Hell-fire! You don't know nothing. The old dam on Ciénega Creek near your grandfather's place went out one night. All the Mexican *jacales* were washed out, and most of the town. The Mexican church went down the river, but Bart Johnson's saloon stood through it all. Ed Hunter was the only white man that suffered. His ranch house was mostly washed down, and Ed drowned trying to save his white-face bulls. His widow took it hard. She took Ellen and moved to her sister's in Marathon. That was when Amory really got under way. He pitched in and said he was going to see this town rebuilt, from the name up. It's now known as Hidalgo."

He went to the door and paused to say sourly: "So you might as well buy your gun permit now as later, because we're the most municipal damned border hole you ever saw. And here I thought you'd come back to turn this dump on its ear!"

Daylight was almost gone when Devlin went out. The cliffs behind the town ran with gaudy reds and mauves. The thin air was clear and dry.

The town now possessed a main street. New buildings had gone up, most of them in the border tradition, with flat roofs and stubby *vigas* instead of eaves. A few had been plastered and whitewashed, and across the way from the Hub was the half-completed shell of a two-story adobe hotel. Down the double line of cottonwood trees were stores, a small, square box with the sign **Post Office, Hidalgo, Texas**, and a nondescript Mexican restaurant.

Devlin entered the restaurant. Its floors were of swept earth and there was a herringbone pattern of willow rods above the ceiling beams. There were several tables and candle-lit booths, in one of which a beardless Mexican youth was playing a zither. Bill Devlin took the seat across from him. He put a dollar on the strings.

"¿Vamos oir 'Chiapanecas', eh?"

The boy played the fast, fluid melody while Bill sang in Spanish. A girl took his order, and the father brought it with an officious thumb in the chili. Things were proceeding *muy amigo* when the newcomer entered.

He was a tall, old man with preoccupied eyes. He sat down at a table and began to roll a cigarette. Bill Devlin

11

had a warm tingling when he recognized him, and not many men could say Devlin had smiled when he saw them. Tom Caslon had been foreman on the Hunter place. Bill's hand went out to still the twang of the strings, and, when it was silent, he said: "Howdy, Tom."

Caslon looked up. He was a lean, old character with a face like a plowed field and eyes like black-glass marbles looking through punctures in the brown skin, a man given to wry jokes and worrying about his health. He peered at the other's dark, smiling face. "Well, Bill!" he said. He came over and took the seat the Mexican boy slid out of.

They shook hands. "I thought you were a general in the Mexican army," Caslon said. "Where's your gold braid and mistresses?"

"Left them at the hotel," Bill said. "Still at the Squared Circle?"

"About decided," said Caslon, "that the circle can't be squared. What've you been doing?"

Bill told him more than he would have told most men. "Oh, I hired for a Mexican railroad, did a year in the army before I bought out, and . . . Well, about everything. I'm playing cards now."

Caslon's smile was touched with wistfulness. "Playing the right cards, too, from the look of you." He looked at Bill's clothes and gold lion's head ring, at the powerful young man's frame that at twenty-five seems indestructible. Bill knew he was not thinking of how much he had grown, but of how old Caslon himself had become.

"I hear Ellen Hunter's back," Bill said.

Caslon nodded and talked gloomily of his attempts to hold the ranch together after her father's death. "She's going to see what she can do herself now. We're down from the ranch to buy some things. She'll stay with one of the women tonight."

"I'll ride up with you as far as your turn-off tomorrow. I ought to say hello to the old man before I leave."

He got that same blank look from Caslon that Johnson had given him when he mentioned his grandfather. Caslon cleared his throat. "You know your grandfather isn't up there any more, don't you? He's across the way."

"In Mexico?" *The old fox must be hiding out*, Bill thought.

Caslon began to cut up his enchilada with a fork. "No. I mean in the cemetery. He died shortly after you left."

"Well, I'll be damned."

Bill was silent a moment, getting used to the idea that he was the last of the line, that old Harry Devlin had shot up the Hub for the last time, that no more would he shout curses at the wolves on Butcherknife Ridge on nights when he had drunk more than usual. "What'd he do, just fade away?" he asked.

Caslon laid down the fork. "Look, Bill. I'll tell you what I know about it, and then don't ask any questions, because you won't get any answers. We had a flood. You heard about it. Ed Hunter was drowned and so were forty Mexicans on their farms in the bottoms. There was some bad feeling when they found out the dam had

13

been dynamited. A gang rode up and found Harry at the dam. They either shot him or lynched him. But either way, he's dead."

All this time Caslon had not looked at him, and now he went on eating quickly and frowningly. Between him and Bill mounted the stiffness Bill remembered from the old days, when he would ride into town to discover his father or grandfather had been raising the devil the night before.

On that ride up from the south, he had leaned on this idea. *The only tie between me and the rest of them is the name.* He denied any relationship to the Devlins of Butcherknife Ridge. He wore good clothes, handmade boots, and rode a horse that not many men in the Bend could have bought. He would let them look at him and then get out.

But his grandfather had scribbled a final, obscene motto on the Devlin escutcheon: *Hanged by a mob!* It threw him off balance. It brought back the sardonic truth that he would never get over a feeling of shame and inadequacy that he had been born north of Butcherknife Ridge.

Caslon was running his thumb around the plate to corral the last of the chili and melted goat's cheese.

Bill chuckled. "He used to buy tamales from Rafaela Sauz down by the river. How he'd yell when he found whiskers in the bacon fat! I'll bet he got tired of it and decided to pay her back. Harry must've forgotten about the rest of them!" Caslon soberly met his eyes, and Bill's grin twisted. He set his palm heavily on the table and leaned forward. "Don't you be giving me any of that!"

Caslon licked his thumb. "Any of what, Bill?"

"Any . . ." Bill's hand groped, but it did not encounter the word. *Pity* was the word in his head, but he'd be damned if he'd say it.

Caslon stood up and left some money by the plate. "Be glad to have you ride out with us, anyway," he said. "You'll be going up there sooner or later for any odds and ends the border-jumpers haven't latched onto."

"Yeah," Bill said. "The silver plate. The rosewood furniture."

Caslon went out.

"Tomaso," Bill said.

"*¿Patrón?*" The Mexican padded across the dirt floor.

"Some red wine," Bill ordered.

The wine looked murky as the Río in May. Bill drank from the neck and began to eat once more. Suddenly the food and the wine became sickening to him, so he paid for his meal and started out. At this point Tom Caslon came back in.

"Thought I'd have a cup of coffee to warm me up, since I've got to sleep out. Johnson says he's rented you the cot."

"Take it," Bill said.

"No, no!" Caslon took his arms and pulled him back to the booth. "Tomaso . . . couple cups of coffee!"

Bill shook his head and started out, but the old man hung onto his arm.

"What's the matter with you?" Bill demanded.

"A cup will do you good," Tom protested.

Bill turned away, then pivoted abruptly. His hand slapped heavily down on Caslon's wrist. He held it, scowling into the old man's eyes, and Caslon released the gun he had pulled from Bill's holster.

"Has everybody in town got to grab at my gun?"

Tom Caslon said: "Al Cheney's in front of the Hub, Bill. He's going to jail you for carrying a gun without a permit."

Whatever it was that made Harry Devlin howl like a wolf when he was on the warpath was bubbling up in Bill now. It was like an artesian well of the best whiskey he ever drank. It was inviting him to drink it, dive in it, swim in it. It said: *You show them, Bill!*

He shook off Caslon's hand and went into the street.

CHAPTER
TWO

Out there the night was warm and full of insects; the black sky was pricked by a million stars. A moist breeze came from the river, carrying the fragrance of plowed earth. In the Hub someone was playing a guitar. Under the wooden awning Devlin saw several men, three of them squatting on their heels, two of them standing. He walked along the uneven dirt path. He passed the squatting men, who looked up, and saw Marshal Cheney beyond the doorway.

Devlin turned in, nodding at Cheney.

"I want to talk to you," Cheney said.

Bill Devlin waited.

"I told you to get a permit before you wore that gun," the marshal said.

Devlin still waited, said nothing. He made money at poker because he understood men, and he knew this man fully and wanted to see how far he would try to bluff his greasy pair of deuces.

Cheney sounded a little hysterical. "You can't come in here bragging that you're the toughest rooster in Texas and not expect trouble! I want that gun."

Bill took off his hat and scratched his head. At the end of the bar, he could see Johnson standing with

17

his face turned toward them. "Did I say I was tough?"

"No, but everything you've done since you hit town has indicated it."

"I'm a law-abiding man," said Bill. "I always try to obey a man elected to a job by due process of law. When were you elected, by the way?"

"Two years ago."

"By the people of Hidalgo?"

Cheney's right hand squeezed tightly and opened slowly. "Charles Amory appointed me."

"Who's Amory to appoint anybody?"

Cheney's breathing was audible. "Amory," he said, "is the man we chose to run out outlaws like you and . . ."

"If you want my gun," Bill said curtly, "you'll have to take it."

He turned back to the door, replacing his hat. In the next moment he fell against the jamb and his arm swept down to slam the heavy brown Stetson into the marshal's face. The men in front of the saloon scrambled across the walk. Cheney, falling backwards and out the door, fired a shot that splintered a window. Bill jumped on him, reaching for his gun and at the same time chopping at his jaw.

He twisted the marshal's gun out of his hand and threw it into the street. The outer wall came up against Cheney's back. He shoved himself away and threw a looping blow at Devlin's face. Bill ducked out of its path and caught the big, blond man by both shoulders. He drove him into the wall once more. He held him there, hammering at his face until Cheney fell away, blood streaming from his nose and lips.

Cheney went to his hands and knees. He shook his head. Heavy drops of blood spattered the dirt. Bill Devlin stood there, sucking a cut knuckle, until Marshal Cheney sat back on his haunches and pushed himself up again. Cheney leaned against the building, blood in his beard, on his shirt, shining on his face. He lurched from the wall.

Bill took a step back. "You don't want any more," he said. "A Devlin may not know much, but he does know how to cut men down to size."

Cheney had had plenty, but some wild sense of pride would not let him quit. He had been a hero in the town's eyes, and now he was being made to look like an ass. He lunged into Bill with a swing that turned his whole body. Bill took the blow on his shoulder. From his hip he brought an uppercut that rammed the marshal's jaws together and tilted his face to the sky.

Cheney made a loose huddle outside of the saloon.

Bill had some drinks after he finished with Cheney. They were like brown fumes in his head the next morning when Bart Johnson woke him. Johnson had a glass in his hand and his ruddy, unshaven face was smiling.

"Bet you ain't too proud to drink my whiskey this morning, Mister Devlin."

Bill reached for it.

"When you get your eyes pried open," said the saloon man, "there's a lady waiting to see you out front."

Bill set down the empty glass. "Why didn't you tell me that first! I look bad enough without having liquor on my breath at eight o'clock in the morning."

"It's eleven," Johnson said.

Bill combed his hair and tested his whiskers with his thumb. He didn't know why it mattered that he had a bruise over his eye, that his clothes were wrinkled from being slept in, and that he stank of liquor and sweat. She was just a girl from the right side of Butcherknife Ridge, but she made him think of pigtails and starched dresses, and of a more gracious life.

He made a small roll of his blankets and some food he bought from Johnson. The sharp sun struck his eyes as he emerged into the street. In an island of shade beneath a cottonwood sat a spring wagon. Tom Caslon was making the flashings tight on the load for the jolting drive up the river. A girl sat on the wagon seat, and even at this distance Bill Devlin knew her.

The topography had changed considerably. The braids and prominent elbows and knees were gone, but the very way she sat identified her. She could put more activity into the mere act of sitting still than anybody he had ever known. The knitting in her lap was merely something to occupy her hands; her attention was with whatever moved within eyesight.

In the old days Bill Devlin had thought she was pretty fine. She always talked to him on the street, which was something most good little girls in the section had been told not to do. And she was still friendly, for she put aside her knitting to wave at him.

"Hello, Bill!" she called.

20

She gave him her hand when he came up. He held it a moment, looking up at her. The sun was in her hair, a rich brown, and its warm tones were in her skin. Bill must have shown his surprise and satisfaction with the changes a few years had made, for she colored a little.

"Throw your bedroll in the back, Bill," she said. "We'll tie your horse on behind."

Bill threw his bedroll into the wagon. He saddled the pony and brought it around. With Ellen Hunter sitting between him and Tom Caslon, they started down toward the river.

They drove past the mud-and-willow huts of the Mexican farmers, close to the river. Ellen gave him an appraising look.

"Bill, I'm disappointed in you."

It gave him a small, adolescent satisfaction that someone should consider him tough. "Somebody had to clean Cheney's plow, sooner or later," he said. "I'm only in town for a few days. Why should I buy a gun permit from a stuffed shirt like Al Cheney?"

"I'm not talking about Al Cheney," Ellen said. "I'm talking about you. Look at you! Look at you! No flowered vest or sideburns, and you're supposed to be a gambler!"

"Who said I was? I just play cards. You save on vests and sleeve guns by not calling yourself a gambler. I'm kind of disappointed in you, too," he told her.

She gave him a questioning look.

"How'd you like the back room at Johnson's?"

A little color warmed her cheeks. "What could I do? Tom and I got there at midnight and I had to be in town in the morning. Anyway, it was a week night and nobody was drinking, and I made Tom sit outside the door."

"It's still sinful," said Bill.

"And that's something, for a Hunter," Ellen remarked.

There was an irony in her inflection that made Bill glance at her.

"The hell-raising Devlins and the sanctimonious Hunters," she said. "There aren't many of us left, Bill. You can hold up your end, but who's going to pray for the wicked and give the deceased a send-off, now that Dad's gone? He should have had a son with a long neck and thick spectacles, instead of a daughter who likes to dance and is unlady-like enough to try to run a ranch."

Bill was a little shocked. Ed Hunter had been the closest thing the area ever had to a preacher. Bill had always respected him for his views, even if his views were hard on the Devlins. "I always thought," he told Ellen, "that Ed was a pretty good man."

"Of course, he was. But I did get tired of being preached at. He should have been a politician, because what he really liked was to orate, and all he could find to orate about in Brewster County was God. Do you know why he was drowned? Because he stayed in the corrals with his bulls, after he'd sent us away, and he defied the waters to touch them. But they did."

The wagon jounced along over the potholes of the river road. They were in a wide and high-walled cañon now, where the river flashed a serpentine course over the sand, and the trees were live oaks growing close to the rim-rock banks.

Ellen smiled. "You know, I always did admire your grandfather for his spirit. All we knew how to do was to sleep, but Harry knew how to wake us up."

Bill drew on his cigarette and looked straight ahead.

"I've always had a theory about the people on the wrong side of the Ridge," Ellen went on. "They acted the way they did because they knew they were expected to. They couldn't just walk into town. Folks would think they were getting soft. And, of course" — she said with a sidelong glance — "a Devlin couldn't knuckle down and buy a permit to carry a gun. He'd have to make some noise about it." She was laughing, but she saw the hard crease between his eyes, and she put her hand on his arm. "Bill, I wasn't being mean . . ."

"Just a lot of good-natured ruffians," Bill said. "Only you haven't explained why Harry murdered your father and forty Mexicans."

She turned her head away, and now it was she who was silent. Suddenly Bill knew what she had been trying to do, and he was sorry he had not been able to go along with it. Frankness was all she understood. She wanted to be friendly, and that meant not talking around subjects that were dark and forbidden ground. So she brought them out and tried to make jokes of them. But what was funny about murder?

CHAPTER
THREE

The low stone parapets of the cañon were broken by a gap on the right, where an arroyo joined the Río. This was Tascosa Creek; the lean backbone of rock rising from the far side of the wash was Butcherknife Ridge. It ran northeast from the river, piling its stones higher every mile, becoming finally a lofty wall between Tascosa Basin and Ciénega Cañon.

In Tascosa Basin, underground stores of water supported colonies of cottonwoods clustered around windmills and earthen tanks. Here and there water filtered to the surface and made a spot of water too large for a pond but too small for a lake. The grass was tobosa and grama and wiry buffalo grass.

There was plenty of water on the wrong side of the Ridge, too, a narrow lagoon of muddy water penned up behind an earthen dam. But water was all there was. The cañon walls tumbled in black ledges to the water. Grass and trees had to hang on with both hands, the ranchers said. It was a lost section of caves and dead-end cañons that bred tough men, horses, and cattle.

A couple of miles up Tascosa Creek, a trail ascended to the heights where the Devlins had reigned, kings of a kingdom nobody else wanted. Bill planned to drop off here and ride up to the old headquarters.

In the stiff silence Ellen asked him: "Are you going back to ranching, Bill?"

"Here? I can starve where the summers are cooler."

Ellen said: "Will you sell me your land then?"

Bill looked at her, seeing by a warmth in her eyes that she had had this in her mind for a long time. He had to smile. "You look like the kind to rope cattle over there, all right."

"Well, I've got to spread out in some direction. We've sold land to Charlie Amory to keep going. You've got one or two spots I could use for winter pasture. I'm serious."

"Got a silver dollar?" Bill asked her.

Tom pulled one out of his pocket. Bill set his teeth down on it, flipped it into the air with his thumbnail, and pocketed it after he caught it. "I'll give you a receipt later," he said.

Ellen looked at him quizzically. "Bill, are you crazy?"

"Don't ever call me sane. You just bought yourself a hundred sections of coyote heaven." The land was virtually unsaleable anyway, unless a man wanted to list it with agents on the outside and hang around a year to show it to buyers.

"Then we'll make it five hundred dollars," Ellen insisted. "This is the down payment, and I'll pay the rest as I can."

The arroyo suddenly opened up. Bill's eyes took in the remembered vista of plain, peak, and ridge, overgrown with grass, here and there a group of trees at a tank. He saw the flash of horns and the slow, red shapes of steers on the flats. There was one note that picked him up sharply. A collection of new buildings sprawled among trees on the right. A line of young trees had been planted on the north, as a windbreak, and a new windmill turned strongly on the north wind.

"Amory's place," Ellen told him. "I'm going by there, unless you want to turn off here."

Bill thought a moment. "No," he said, "I'll go with you."

Bill Devlin noticed that everyone referred to the senator from Brewster County as Amory, or Charlie Amory. In his day it had been Big Charlie.

Big Charlie owned a small ranch east of Mariscal Cañon. There was always a wind over there, and perhaps that was how Big Charlie learned to make speeches, by shouting over the wind at his cowpunchers. He had a fine, deep-chested figure and iron-gray hair, and he was outstanding in the saddle or on a platform.

As county supervisor he promised to build a good road into the Bend, and one was actually started. Perhaps it was on the contract from this job that he made enough money to buy a larger ranch. He could have moved outside, where the opportunities were greater, but he was loyal to his own people, and there he stayed, until he moved to Austin, and later to Washington. Now he was back, and some of the plush seemed to have rubbed off on him.

The Spade Ranch was like a picture from a stockman's catalogue, with white buildings, stately old shade trees, neat pole corrals, barns, an adobe ranch house with a long porch, and *vigas* tempting anyone who needed a place to hang a string of chilis to dry or a water jug to sweat in the shade. Workmen and cowpunchers came and went like soldiers in an army camp.

They stopped in the yard. Onto the porch strode a portly figure in a black box coat and gray-checkered pants. His hair was white. But it was Big Charlie's voice, the hunting-dog voice that sounded as if he shouted too much. "Bill Devlin! Sure, it's good to see you!"

On the steps, Amory offered his hand as though he were presenting a gold watch to a faithful employee. "Bill, how are you?" he asked.

"Fine. How you been, Senator?"

"Forget I was ever a lawmaker, Bill. It's plain Charlie now. We're just sitting down to eat a bite. Come in, all of you."

He was a windbag, Bill decided, but a forceful windbag, aggressive and commanding. He had a strong brow and a thick-nosed, bearded face. He kept his beard close-cut, and, now that it had gone white, he looked like a middle-aged Robert E. Lee.

Mrs. Amory was already at the table with Jarco and Amory's foreman, Ostrander. She was an ineffectual, gray little woman who worshipped her husband. She used to talk about "the senator", but now it was "Mister Amory".

27

Bill sat at Amory's right. Jarco was at the left, looking ill at ease. Bill could guess why he had come out to the ranch so early. He said: "How's Cheney?"

Jarco grinned his habitually nervous smile. "All right," he said. He took a paper from his pocket and thrust it across the table. "Here."

Bill looked at it. It was a permit to carry a gun, signed by Cheney. He left it lying on the cloth. "I don't need it," he said.

Petulant anger flashed in Jarco's eyes. "Listen here, Devlin . . ."

Amory patted the table three times with his broad palm. Jarco shut up. "Bill, I hate to see you acting like a schoolboy. I've squared things with Marshal Cheney for you. Now, let's forget the whole thing."

He smiled at Bill, and Bill smiled at him, and the paper lay between them. "I've never been much of a joiner," Bill said.

Amory's reaction was not anger. It was a sandbagged incomprehension. But he was a good general, and neither withdrew his forces nor thrust them into an untenable position. He let the paper remain where it was.

Bill changed the subject. "Why did you leave Washington, Charlie?"

Again Amory's heavy-browed eyes showed displeasure. He considered it a moment, and then spoke sincerely, almost wistfully. "I got sick, Bill. I almost died." His fist tapped his chest. "The doctor said I wouldn't be able to fight those Washington lobbyists for a long time, so I came home."

Bill murmured something, but Amory had turned to Caslon. "Tom, I've got a bone to pick with you. Didn't you hire a Mexican last week?"

Caslon, a shy man who spoke with difficulty before so many people, muttered: "Couldn't find a good white man, Mister Amory."

Ostrander, Amory's foreman, snorted. "Don't give us that, Tom. There are plenty of men right in town." Ostrander was a stoutly built man of middle height with dark skin. He wore a wide mustache like a strip of black tape across his lip.

"Tom said *good* men," Ellen pointed out.

"Even so," Amory contended, "he should have waited. This land belongs to the sons of the pioneers who wrested it from the Mexicans. Why should we raise a finger to help a foreigner?"

Ellen spoke tartly. "This was to help us, not them. He's not a wetback. He's a citizen."

"I think," Amory said, "it would be a good idea to replace him as soon as possible."

Ellen did not get excited, but she spoke as flatly as any man in an argument. "I may have to hire a dozen more Mexicans, as far as that goes. I've just bought some more land."

Amory looked up, surprise easing the lines of displeasure in his face.

"Bill's ranch," Ellen explained. "We made a deal on the way up."

Amory chuckled softly. "But it wasn't Bill's to sell."

"Whose was it?" Bill demanded.

"The people's. I had the title changed after the flood. There were so many lawsuits against Harry Devlin's estate, any one of which would have won a judgment, that I had the land declared public property."

Bill rubbed his neck, beginning to grin. "I suppose I ought to be sore. It's kind of funny, though, when you've been away and come back to find a minstrel show going on like this. You appointed Cheney. You declared the land public property. If you don't mind my asking, Senator, who the hell are you . . . Abraham Lincoln?"

There was a rustle of movement at the other end of the table. Mrs. Amory was on her feet, a mouse roused to fury. "Young man, you are a guest at Mister Amory's table!"

"I guess that's so," Bill said. "But what of it?"

Amory arose. "Shall we go outside, gentlemen?"

They went outside, the gentlemen and Ellen. Ostrander stood there with his feet set widely, glowering at Bill. Color had come up in Amory's vein-threaded cheeks. There was a special tremolo in his voice.

"Let's understand each other, Devlin. Two things have taken place since you left. Your grandfather was hung for murder, and we've set out to make the Big Bend something more than the back door of Texas. Our legislative methods may be primitive, but we've accomplished more in four years than those pettifogging politicians in Washington will in the next forty."

Bill held onto one word from the speech. He said: "How do you know he was hung?"

Amory stared. "I've heard the story told a dozen ways. We've always assumed a lynching party had something to do with his death. Does it matter?"

"Did it occur to anybody that somebody else might have done the dynamiting?"

"As a matter of fact," Amory said stonily, "I wasn't pleased myself by the lynching. I had an investigation made. I was convinced then that the right man had been punished."

"If it had been anybody but my grandfather, he'd have been given a trial before he was lynched, instead of after. Isn't that right?"

Ostrander snorted. "If you were anyone but a Devlin, you'd know that only a drunken old goat like your grandfather would have done it. Or your father."

A kind of a thrill ran through Bill, a trumpet singing in him. Talk about the sober life all you wanted — but try to match the gusto of a fight. He looked at Ostrander's sanctimonious, sneering face, and he knew he was going to change it.

Amory roared something as Bill reached for the foreman, but Ostrander stood there as if he thought his employer's presence gave him some kind of immunity. Bill yanked him close by the tags of his string tie. He struck him once, a staggering blow that came down on the bridge of his nose. He let him go. Ostrander's hand covered his nose and eyes, and he moved blindly toward the wall, and leaned there breathing in a kind of labored panting. Bill watched him; it was a punch he liked, which would cut down the biggest.

31

Jarco was piping: "Bill, you ain't got the sense the Lord gave a hoot owl! Twenty-four hours in town and you pick two fights!"

Bill grinned. "You didn't think I came back to join the church, did you? Senator," he continued, turning, "you'd better get that title changed on the books. The land belongs to Miss Hunter, but I may stay around long enough to be sure you haven't got any more two-gun marshals pastured up there."

At a nest of red boulders lying against the foot of Butcherknife Ridge, Bill untied his horse.

"It's just something about you, Bill," Ellen said. "They can't help throwing their weight around."

"I'll be coming up there to run a count on the cattle," Caslon said. "You hear about the ruckus up on the ridge?"

Bill mounted. "I haven't heard about anything," he said.

"Well, you remember Mariano Mata, your grandfather's old sidekick? At least," he amended hastily, "they seemed to be pretty friendly."

"They were friendly," Bill agreed. "Mariano used to run wet cattle from Coahuila up to the States, pick up a bunch of American cattle, and take them back. The Mexican always drove them up Ciñega Cañon where, for a price, he could count on Harry Devlin's not noticing him."

"Mariano moved in a few boys after Harry died, to kind of watch things for him. It got to Amory. He knows a lot of us leave a few bucks in a hollow tree where Mariano will find it, now and then, just to keep off the curse. So he sent up a bunch of his 'punchers one night and they spotted two of the Mexicans and killed them. I thought you ought to know," Caslon said.

"Thanks," Bill replied.

Ellen stood up in the wagon, her arm up to shield her face from the sun. She was a slender, slim-waisted figure with long, dark hair lying softly on her shoulders. She made Bill think of a mountain alder beside a stream, straight and clean.

"Take care, Bill," she said, and smiled.

Bill raised his hand and grinned back.

From above, twenty minutes later, he looked down on the wagon following the arroyo. He thought of some girls he had known, colorful, provocative girls who knew how the game was played. At the time he had thought they were the only kind to have. The beginning and the end were all up to you. He began now to have some inkling that there were deficiencies in that kind of love. Love could be a slow stream moving gently, as well as a headlong rapid. He thought with a jolt: *Look out, Bill! Don't spoil your taste for bad women, the way you did for bad whiskey.*

CHAPTER
FOUR

Across the ridge and a quarter mile down, a rocky shoulder thrust out from the mountain. It was perhaps a half mile long and provided hold for a few mean adobes, stone corrals, and a smoke house. Elsewhere it was rough with cairns of black rock tufted with dry yellow grass and overgrown with low oaks that lay flat along the cliff.

Harry Devlin had named the spot El Miradero, The Lookout. He had balanced his cabin on the brink of the cliff and placed an extra slotted box atop it as a conning tower. The old weed-grown headquarters had the melancholy look of a graveyard. The corrals were empty; the doors hung crookedly on rawhide hinges. The constant wind, sweeping up from the cañon floor, flapped a shutter.

Bill turned the horse into the corral, unsaddled, carried his bedroll into the cabin, and took stock. On the floors, pack rats had deposited their little offerings of twigs and piñon husks. Coyotes had left their tracks in the dust. But the air, sweeping through the unglazed windows, was clean and fresh.

Dusk was coming on. Bill made a fire in one of the sections of the Mexican-style cook stove. He sat on the porch to eat and watch the shadows invade the cañons. Tascosa Cañon, with its dam and serpentine brown lake, was a deep, twisting slice through the mountains. The run-off from the dam swung around the back to enter Tascosa Basin. The thousand feeder cañons angling into the mother cañon were unnamed barrancas where cattle hid and grew tough as the shrubs they fed on. A king might have selected a spot like this for his castle, except that there was nothing to rule but buzzards, coyotes, and rattlers.

For the first time in his life, Bill began to notice some things about the cabin. It started with the porch rail. He had his feet up on it, and, as he crossed his boots, he noticed that the cottonwood pole was carved. A design borrowed from Harry Devlin's Gourd Vine cattle brand turned the whole length of it, interspersed with a sort of Aztec monogram of his initials.

A small door into the mind of his grandfather opened up. It was a startling thing to discover that the old wolf had had any appreciation whatever for ornament. Then he remembered the books he used to read, Scott and Tennyson, Milton, Omar Khayyam and Shakespeare. He always read aloud, the rolling music of his voice awaking echoes.

It had not occurred to Bill to wonder where he had learned to read. But what little reading matter was blown down here to the Bend by the winds, he devoured — even the *Congressional Record*, which Senator Amory mailed to his constituents whenever he had a speech in it. Harry considered these masterpieces of imbecility.

"Lord Almighty!" he would shout. "Listen to this . . . 'Senator Amory . . . I wish to call my honored colleague's attention to the fact that the Big Bend of Texas is not a desert, as he has pictured it in speaking against my bill, but literally a bower of flowers. At night, the soft Texas sky is gemmed with baubles of the night, which speed their circling flight over cañons lush with verdure and . . . ' Is the damned fool talking about Texas?"

Bill could see the old man more clearly through the distance of the years, than he could before, when he had had his violent tempers, his drunkenness, and his filth to put up with. There was something melancholy in the picture of him. It came to Bill that he must have been pretty drunk to have thought of dynamiting the dam. And if he were that drunk, how had he made his way down there over five miles of twisting mountain trail without sobering up?

In the heavy dusk he lit a cigarette and rose to go into the cabin. Something slapped the porch rail, tearing splinters from it and leaving a pale scar on the round surface. He stood staring at it, not understanding that he had been shot at.

Then a great lump of fear seemed to bounce up in his throat, jarring him. He fell back toward the door. A second shot thunked against the adobe wall at his left, just as the echoes of the first poured down the cliffs.

Bill stumbled inside. His saddle gun leaned against the wall by the door. Through the rear windows spat a fusillade of rifle balls. In the almost dark cabin they ricocheted terrifyingly. To reach the tower, it was necessary to cross the room. He got down on his hands and knees and made it to the ladder.

The rungs were loose on their pegs, but he climbed to the trap door, thrust it open, and won the roofless tower. He pressed against the thick mud and sighted through one of the rifle loops. Out there he saw a spurt of flame in a tangle of cholla and pulled a bead. The slug went into a cactus and wailed off a rock.

After this, the fire was at the tower instead of the cabin. He pressed back against the wall between two of the loops. A bullet would hammer the edge of a slot, kick a handful of grit inside, and sometimes roll upon the floor. Bill had some profane thoughts about Charles Amory.

Again he peered out. Soon the landmarks would be one soundless shadow, but in that shadow other shadows would move. Bill heard a spur chime briefly behind the stone wall of the corral. He fired at the sound, and then, because his rage and frustration were too much to contain, he shouted: "Come and get me! *¡Alcahuete cabrón!*" It took two languages to express what he felt.

There was a ringing silence. Then a head showed imprudently above the wall. A thick Mexican voice called: "Hey! That *Don* Beel?"

Emotion ran out of Bill like grain through a hole in a sack. He leaned against the wall and laughed. He put his mouth to a loop. "It ain't Amory! Come on in, Mariano!"

There were ten of them. They crowded into the cabin, bringing their gusto and their smells and their white-toothed grins with them. One carried a sack of food that he took into the kitchen. In the Mexican style, Bill and the outlaw, Mariano Mata, threw their arms about each other and pounded one another on the back, while they lied about how much each had been missed.

Mata had become grossly stout. Bill remembered him as a vigorous man in his forties, getting heavy but still a figure to catch a girl's eye, strong, big-shouldered, smiling. He and Harry would yarn on the porch for an hour or two, and then Bill would be sent to bed and a deal would be made.

Now his cheeks were fat and his eyes bleary, his unshaven beard had a peppering of gray. His belly made his enormous shoulders less impressive. But he had his old heartiness and talked rapidly in *cholo*.

"I been watching this place, Beel. I theenk *mañana* I get one of those fellas. You know w'at they do to Carlito?"

"I heard about it."

"But you don't know w'at I gonna do to somebody I catch. I no keel him, oh, no! In Coahuila, the ants are lions, the honey is sweet. Stake a man out, put leetle honey in his eyes, and . . ."

"I get the idea," Bill said.

Mariano nudged him and guffawed. "I weesh you see him keek!"

The cook brought a stack of tortillas and a pan of chili from the kitchen. The outlaws grabbed tortillas, rolled them, sopped them in the thin chili sauce. They sat at the table or against the wall to eat.

"How's business?" Bill asked the Mexican.

Mata shrugged. "*Asi, asi*. I work leetle deef'rent, now. Used to breeng leetle bonch of cows up from the south, sell them in the north, take leetle bonch back. Now I say to rancher . . . 'Somebody gonna steal some your cows, *patrón*. For so much I make him leave them be.' He pays me, don' lose so much, I don't have to work so hard."

Bill looked at his paunch. "I saw that right away."

Mata slapped his belly. "We ought to have some wine, *hombre*."

"I know where Harry used to keep it. It's probably vinegar by now, providing there's any left." He took a candle, gnawed by the rats, and Mariano accompanied him to the kitchen. Bill raised a trap in the floor. He heard rats scurry and saw a flash of small, evil eyes. He went down six stairs to the floor. On shelves dug into the hard earth, there were still a number of bottles. Bill got an armful, saw a fifth of mescal, and brought that, too.

The wine was fair. Mata's men clamored over the mescal, which Bill began to pour, a little into each pottery cup. The bottle was dusty, and because of this he did not see the thing in it until he had nearly finished pouring. It floated into the neck, and Bill looked at a man's thumb, white as tallow except for a crescent of dirt under the nail. One of the men, who had already drunk his liquor, saw it and doubled over and began to vomit.

"Good Lord!" Bill said.

Mata roared with laughter as half the men became sick. He took the bottle from Bill and rubbed some of the dust off with his sleeve. "Fonny lookin' thumb. Kinda flat, hennit?"

"Yeah," Bill said. "It sure is."

Jarco's thumbs were flat and out-curving, almost his sole mark of the dwarf. And the thumb on his left hand was missing, a carpentry casualty Bill had thought.

"Enrique" — Mata chuckled — "hav' a helluva sense of humor, eh?"

Bill's thoughts were venturing along a dim corridor, at the end of which something was dimly seen. He sat down and smoked while the rest ate. He said at last: "I wonder whose idea it was to lynch him?"

"Amory's, I guess. Maybe it was Amory's idea to blow up the dam, too. Lots of my people down in the bottoms those days. Good people, but good people drown jus' as quick as anybody else. You theenk he let *Mejicanos* settle there again? *¡Eso!*"

"He'd be afraid to do that. He hasn't the guts to be a killer."

"Anybody has, eef he have to."

Bill reflected. Mariano was right. Terror bred strong men. Did the thumb of Jarco make its possessor dangerous enough to kill? Bill couldn't see how.

The wine began to rouse unpleasant thoughts in the Mexican. He held a tortilla before him and with a pocket knife sliced thin strips from it. "Someday I'm coming through Chito just like the army of Juárez. I don' like that fella, Amory. I'm getting old, Beel, I'm

40

going to retire *poco tiempo*, but first I let him feel the weight of my heel."

He put a heel on the floor and worked it back and forth. Then he sighed. "When old Enrique was here, all was *todo bueno*. No trobble."

Bill grunted.

Mata glanced at him. "You didn't like him so much then, eh, Beel?"

"He was tough to get along with."

"Too bad you didn't know him as a man, instead of an *abuelo*. He was much of a man." He put the bottle to his lips, drank, wiped the back of his hand across his mouth. "W'at you do now, *hombre?*"

Bill told him about selling the ranch. "I'll stay here a while to try to straighten Amory out on the idea that he can hook onto this iron. By the way, do you ever see any of Ellen Hunter's Squared Circle cattle down there?"

Mariano looked at the ceiling. "Two, three, now and then."

Bill had some money in a bank in Laredo. He had brought an additional sum with him, in gold, for you never knew when a game would stand up and beckon you. He had a double reason for wanting to strengthen Ellen's position — to bring one of the old ranches back, and to weaken Amory's hold. Now he perceived a way to do it. He asked the Mexican: "For two dollars a head do you think you could find five hundred of them?"

Mata showed his stained teeth. "I know where to look, *amigo*. When do you want them?"

"Make it Saturday."

"*De acuerdo.* You know Sombrero Peak? I meet you there." Mata drank his wine. "She's *muy bonita,* no?"

Bill shrugged. "Ellen? I suppose so. Why?"

Mariano laughed. "You and me, we work deef'rent. I see a girl. I take her. You buy her a herd of cattle and say to yourself, maybe she decide I'm not soch a bad fella."

"Go to hell," Bill said, grinning.

Mata decided to spend part of the night at El Miradero. He sent two men out as guards, letting the rest wrap themselves in their *zarapes* to sleep a few hours. Bill shook the dust out of his old cot and made his bed on it.

CHAPTER
FIVE

In the morning, after the Mexicans left, he lay around, smoking, poking into dusty corners of the buildings, sprawling on the porch in a deep, rawhide chair. Again he thought of the thumb, wondering how Harry had got hold of the grisly trophy, and why it wasn't known in Hidalgo. At any rate, it was worth keeping. Bill wondered whether the inch or two of mescal remaining in the bottle would be enough to preserve it.

He lit a candle and carried the bottle to the cellar. He inspected the bottles still in their musty beds until he located another fifth of mescal. He added the contents of this to the first, bringing the level almost to the top. As a precaution, he moved a few bottles away and reached behind them to deposit the other in a place of safety.

His hand failed to encounter the back of the shelf. He kept reaching, and suddenly, on feeling the bottle strike metal, he withdrew his hand. A coldness ran through him. He thrust the candle into the opening he had made. Then he leaned weakly against the wall for a moment and swallowed a lump of panic.

A rusty trap the length of one of his boots yawned in the hole. So this was how Jarco left his thumb behind!

He, too, must have been looking for Harry Devlin's strongbox. But Jarco had had no right to be there.

Some old boards lay in a corner. With one of them, Bill set off the trap. He pulled it out and found a chain coupling it to a ring in a facing of rock at the back of the hole. There was a tin strongbox inside, with a padlock and a rusty hasp that he knocked off with a hammer.

In the weak light of the candle, he looked at the sheaves of bills, mostly Mexican goldbacks half the size of a saddle blanket. The rest were American currency. Bill carried the box upstairs, shaky with buried-treasure fever. He placed it on the table, and then climbed to the tower to scan the area about the cabin.

After this he spread the money on the table. He took one look at the Mexican goldbacks, and the breath went out of him. They were currency of the Second Empire under Maximilian. They were worthless. Diaz liked his own money.

The American currency amounted to some thirty-five hundred dollars. This would be the money Mariano Mata left on his return trips. Bill leaned back in the chair and drummed his fingers on the table, the thrill of sudden wealth burning in him. On an impulse, he turned the strongbox over and shook it. Nothing fell out but the newspaper that had underlain the money as a lining.

It was an ancient copy of the *Congressional Record* of a date four years past. Bill was a little curious as to why Harry had employed it for this purpose; he had always maintained there was only one use for Amory's speeches, and he had used them to start fires. Bill glanced down the columns until he found Amory's name. Amory had made a highfaluting encomium on the Big Bend of Texas, in connection with a million dollars he was asking for roads and a port of entry on the Rio Grande at Chito. At the conclusion, a Senator Rowley had made rebuttal.

Senator Rowley: It seems to me Senator Amory is almighty interested in the welfare of one section of Texas, to the detriment of the rest of the Union.

Senator Amory: My honored colleague entirely misses the point. The Big Bend is an important factor in the economic welfare of Texas. A lot of us have money invested down there.

Senator Rowley: Oh! Then it is Senator Amory's welfare he has in mind, rather than that of Texas? (*Laughter*)

After that, it became rather brutal. Rowley was a fast-thinking, experienced politician who verbally knocked Amory down, picked him up, kicked him, and had the gallery roaring at the Texan's confusion. Bill felt uncomfortable, the way he did when he heard a speaker forget his lines. He thought of the pompous Amory, the big frog from the small puddle, floundering miserably in a puddle too big for him.

Senator Amory: Perhaps your inference that I intend to request the Big Bend to secede from the

45

Union is no joke, Senator. Perhaps the idea isn't so bad, if this is the way her interests are protected.

Senator Rowley: Gentlemen, I hope you are listening closely. I believe this is the first time secession has been mentioned since 1860. Mr. Secretary, I submit that the senator should be held to account for that remark.

Secretary: Has Senator Amory anything to say?

Senator Amory hereupon left the floor.

Bill Devlin had the uncomfortable sensation of having seen a surgeon bungle an operation. A scalpel had been plunged into Charlie Amory's mind, but instead of a neat job of resection, it had slashed and twisted. He saw Amory's bearded face, the eyes earnest. *I was sick, Bill. I almost died.* But now he knew Amory's body had not been sick, but his mind. Down here his opposition had all been fourth-rate. He had grown complacent on victory, and in that state of mind he had stepped confidently onto the floor of the Senate and been made to look a complete fool.

He had crawled miserably home. But before long his soul, craving flattery and power, began to try its bruised limbs again. It would have started with boasting talk in the Hub probably, quasi-political talks in the barbershop, touting a school, a church, better irrigation, anything that was sure-fire. And then the flood came . . .

That must have been what gave him the shove. Chito needed him. Bill thought of how it would have gone. *On the ruins of the old town we shall build anew, build to a glorious future!*

The flood was the only favor Harry Devlin had ever done Charlie Amory. Harry liked to argue politics with Big Charlie. He would always make a fool of him, but inevitably it terminated in Harry's getting abusive, and he lost sight of his point in vituperation. But the flood made up for everything. It took Harry out of the way. It gave Amory a springboard to power. It wasn't often fate pampered a man like that. Usually he had to make the arrangements himself.

For the first time, Bill began to wish he had known something about his grandfather. He couldn't fit him into this dynamiting business. He couldn't see a man of Harry Devlin's frank, if unpleasant, temperament getting cagey that way. If he had wanted to kill forty Mexicans, he would have taken a rifle and a box of shells and gone after them. Why couldn't Amory have done it himself?

Bill walked up and down the porch and smoked, and decided it was out of character for Amory, too. He wasn't too direct for it, but he was too cautious. And anyway, the land didn't amount to more than a few hundred acres and was a mere by-product of the accident. Just as the hanging of his grandfather was a by-product.

From too much wondering about too many angles, Bill began to feel weary. He saddled and rode down the Ciénega Cañon trail.

Until Thursday night, he rode the cañons, making a range count of the cattle. There weren't many left. These had become as wild as wolves, too tough to rope or eat. But on the meadows where Tascosa and Ciénega Creeks started, the grass was deep. It would make good winter pasture for Squared Circle.

Friday morning he put some crackers and sardines in a saddlebag and started for Tascosa Basin. He had said nothing to Ellen about the shipment of cattle she was going to receive tomorrow night; he would need a few of her cowpunchers to help drive them in. But this was only one reason for riding down. Bill Devlin had some questions he wanted to ask Bart Johnson about his grandfather.

He was about halfway down when he saw a horse and rider below him. He pulled off behind some boulders and waited, but, as the rider came into view, he saw that it was Ellen. She had never been too proud to wear a man's clothes when she went riding, and he saw now that she wore denims, boots, and a checkered shirt. She hadn't seen him, and he dismounted quietly with his saddle gun in his hand. He let her reach the rocks. Then he said: "*¡Hay no más, Chata!*"

Her head jerked around; he had a glimpse of the startled oval of her face. Then she relaxed and exhaled her breath.

"Bill, you darned fool! What are you doing . . . playing badman?"

"No, but some guys up here have been. If you aren't afraid of Mariano Mata, you ought to be afraid of Comanches. And if you aren't afraid of them, you ought to be afraid of me."

She dismounted and led her horse into the shade beside Bill's pony. She sat down, leaned back on her

48

outspread hands, and shook out her hair. "I'm not afraid of Mexicans and Indians," she said, "and we'll see how I make out with you."

Bill sat down. He felt at ease with her, somehow exhilarated. Everything seemed sharper, like a vista of trees and water through autumn light. "Hunting your own strays now?" he asked her.

"I was on my way up to see you. Sorry you sold the ranch?"

"I was a fool," Bill said darkly. "I should have held out for two dollars."

She laughed, and then there was a pause. "It wasn't just a social call," she said. "There's something new about Amory. I'm not going to be running to you every time there's any trouble, Bill, but this concerns you, too. He served an injunction on me yesterday not to trespass on the Gourd Vine."

"He's going to try to make it stick, is he?"

"Apparently. And besides, Tom learned something in town yesterday. Cheney's deputized some of Amory's men to help him take you if you show up wearing a gun. You made a mistake when you wouldn't take that permit Amory offered you. You've put the whole bunch of them in a position they can't tolerate. You've made fools of them."

"Somebody else did that," Bill said. "I just pointed it out to them. They'll want to hang me when they hear that I made a deal with Mata the other day! You've got five hundred cattle coming up tomorrow night. I was going to get Tom to help bring them across."

"Stolen cattle?"

"Not exactly. They were stolen from you, to begin with. I'm paying Mariano two bucks a head to bring them back."

Ellen put a hand to her cheek. "Bill, I don't know whether to kiss you or turn you over to the law. I can't pay for those cattle. And I can't go into debt any more than I already am."

"I'll tell you a secret," Bill said. "I found thirty-five hundred dollars in the cellar. I'm splitting it with you, though it's legally yours."

She just looked at him for a while. "Why are you doing all this for me, Bill? You've known girls. It's not as though you were standing on your hands to impress the first girl you'd ever met."

"It's pretty close to that," Bill admitted. "I'm doing it for another kid. He used to live up in Butcherknife Ridge, a tough, dirty little *hombre* who had quite a case on you. He was always making a hair bridle or carving an eagle out of a cow's horn to give you, but he didn't have the nerve to do it. A good thing he didn't, too. Your old man would have whaled the daylights out of him. Anyway, this is one of the hair bridles he made you. And you're welcome."

Women are queer, Bill thought. She lay back against the slope with her arm across her forehead, looking at him in a way no woman ever had, and there were tears in her eyes. "You sound as though you were talking about somebody else," she said.

"I am. This kid ran away from home and never came back. Somebody else came back, so, if I feel sorry for him, it isn't really self-pity."

When he looked down at her again, she had closed her eyes. He noticed the faint blue shadows under her eyes and the thin lines of her nose, and, when his shadow fell across her, her face relaxed and the lips softened.

It was a restrained sort of kiss. Afterward she looked up, without stirring, but with a smile. "You shouldn't have done that, Bill."

"I know it," Bill said.

He kissed her more thoroughly this time. Suddenly his fingers curved around her head, pulled her mouth hard against his. That ended it. She pushed him away and sat up.

"You really shouldn't have done that!" She got up, brushed the dirt off her Levi's, and walked to her pony.

When she mounted and started down the trail, Bill followed her. They reached the creek. She gave him a stern look as he rode up beside her. "The Devlins are all the same."

"Always in somebody else's pasture," Bill agreed.

Ellen's brows went up. "Whose pasture am I supposed to be in?"

"I don't know. But not mine. Bill Smith's or Bill Jones's, but not Bill Devlin's." It sounded gruff, and he started to embroider the remark. Then he knew he couldn't, and shut up. The women of the Devlin tribe didn't have a pleasant time of it. They got a little breathless trying to keep up, and finally decided it wasn't worth the effort and quit. Ellen deserved something better than that out of marriage.

She did not refer to it again. Perhaps she remembered the last time she had tried to talk about the Devlins' place in society.

At the fork, they separated. Bill told her to have Tom Caslon meet him with four or five boys at Sombrero Peak the next afternoon. Then he swung his pony toward town. Ellen called him.

"Bill, you're not going into Hidalgo!"

He nodded. "Things to do."

She shook her head impatiently. "You don't need to go out of your way to look for trouble. It finds you soon enough, it seems to me."

Bill rode on. He was almost sorry he hadn't accepted the permit Amory wanted to give him, because now he wanted freedom of movement, and they weren't going to give it to him. And he knew the answer to his going in unarmed. They had the scruples of a pack of timber wolves. Nothing but the threat of a gun would keep them in line now.

He had Amory on the run. That conviction was growing in him. Big Charlie had had the cards stacked just the way he wanted them. He was the big dealer, and he dealt and played the cards the way he wanted. Along came a blue-jawed rough-neck who wanted the deal to change. Whatever Charlie Amory had been ten years ago, he was now a man who had to be the boss.

Bill reached the wide, sandy wash of the Big River. He let the pony walk into the hollow stream and poke its muzzle in the water. He wondered how many times Harry Devlin had stopped at this same spot to water his horse. It was a curious thing that, when he thought of his grandfather now, it was no longer with sourness. It was with curiosity to know what kind of man he had been underneath the crust.

There was a thing Bill had to get straightened out. Whether — and why — Harry had caused the death of those Mexicans.

CHAPTER
SIX

It was mid-afternoon when he came from the *bosque* into the green of the farmlands. He reached the double line of cottonwoods at the head of town and stopped a moment to gaze along it. There was a special feeling of activity. It was Saturday. Mexicans were in with ox carts heaped with dripping loads of produce. Ranch and townswomen in their long cotton dresses and sunbonnets were talking on the sidewalks.

Bill didn't see Cheney as he rode in. He saw a lot of Spade cowpunchers. They gave him quick, startled looks and got busy rolling cigarettes or inspecting saddle cinches. Before the Hub he found a disconsolate crowd sitting under the awning. Bart Johnson was among them, a big, red-faced figure sprawled on the bench with his legs stretched across the walk.

Bill looked at the padlocked door. "What the devil are you doing? Those men look thirsty."

"I'm locked up."

"Well, unlock," Bill ordered.

"Cheney's got the key." Bart Johnson rolled his head disgustedly. "I threw Jarco out last night. The damn' little wart got drunk and shot off his mouth about a lot of changes he was going to make, including a tax on each drink sold in town. When he's drunk, I can't go him."

Bill dismounted and dropped the reins of his pony across the rack. When Johnson saw him take out his gun, he got up quickly.

"Bill, you're in enough trouble! Let me handle this one."

The Colt bucked in Bill's hand; the padlock leaped. It was no longer a padlock, but a tangle of bent brass. He pushed the door open. "See if you can't find me something besides that Mexican bellywash, Bart."

After Johnson had taken care of everybody, Bill went outside and returned with a bottle that he set on the bar. It was the bottle of mescal. Bart peered at the white thumb floating in it. "Where in the hell did you get that?" he demanded.

"Ever seen one like it?"

Johnson handled the bottle as though it contained a tarantula. He said speculatively: "Yeah. Only the one I saw was on somebody's hand. He hasn't got one on his other hand."

Bill set it behind the bar. He leaned on the varnished pine to punch the burned shell out of his gun and replaced it. "You knew Harry about as well as anybody," he said. "What did you think about his blowing up the dam?"

Johnson wiped the bar with a towel. "Well, I always thought it wasn't much like him."

"How were he and Amory getting along when it happened?"

"How did they get along? Rotten. Funny thing," Johnson said, squinting, "one night, after they'd wrangled about religion, women, and politics, Harry said . . . 'Senator, I'd like to challenge you to a debate.'"

"'Any time,' Charlie says. 'On what subject?'"

"'On the question of whether the Big Bend should secede from the Union.' Bill, you never saw such a look on a man's face! It was like Charlie'd heard a horse come in here and ask for a shot of whiskey. Now, why should a thing like that throw him?"

There was a coolness and a burning in Bill. "Hadn't you ever heard secession mentioned before?"

"Why should I have?"

"Didn't Amory send you the *Congressional Record* whenever he had a speech in it?"

"Sure. Didn't read it very often, though."

"And you never read a speech of his where he suggested the Big Bend secede from the Union? Never heard anybody else mention reading it?"

"No."

"Well," Bill said, "I found a copy of a speech he made where he suggested it. Know what I think? That only one copy of that paper got mailed down here, and of all people it was mailed to Harry! Bart, it wasn't the kind of speech he'd have sent home on purpose. Some other senator made a fool out of him. It was murder. My guess is that one of his clerks sent out just one copy, by accident."

Johnson had to wait on a couple of customers. When he came back, he looked puzzled and indignant. "What kind of a maniac is he, to suggest a thing like that? He made a fool out of the Bend, as well as himself."

"I've got a notion he was only half serious at the time. But after they ran him out of Washington, it must have begun to work on him. I don't think he really believes he could make an independent republic out of a few hundred white men and a thousand Mexicans, but ... well, he likes to dream about it. And he couldn't run things any tighter down here if he *was* President!"

"That's a fact. When they can lock a man up for bouncing a drunk! It wasn't that way in your granddaddy's day," Johnson said abruptly. "Say, I think I've got something of his in here." He unlocked a cupboard behind the bar and lugged out a vast, calf-bound Bible. He placed it on the bar and began to dust it. "I took it in on a liquor bill once. He never redeemed it, but sometimes he'd ask me to get it out so's he could read it. Ever hear him read the Bible, Bill? By the Almighty, it was fit to make your flesh crawl!"

Bill turned the pages. He came to some parchment pages with ruled lines, on some of which were entries in careful, copperplate script. At the top were the headings: **Births — Marriages — Deaths.** Harry's was the first name on the **Births** page. Something seemed to take him by the throat. He had never seen his grandfather's name in writing before.

Henry Thomas Devlin, Litt. B., LL. D., born Feb. 25, 1806, Troy, N.Y. Married Sarah Lawrence Bailey, Nov. 4, 1839. Children: John Milton Devlin,

b. July 2, 1841. Grandchildren: William Makepeace Devlin, b. 1860.

There were two entries on the **Deaths** page: **Sarah Bailey Devlin, beloved wife of Henry** — Bill's grandmother. He noticed that the date of her death was that of his father's birth. His father's name was entered under **Deaths** in 1863. **At Chancellorsville,** it said.

Bill mused. So John Milton Devlin had never come back from the war, and old Henry Thomas Devlin was saddled with a kid who was bound to interfere with his drinking. Johnson looked a little awed by the effect it had made on Bill.

Bill rubbed his hand carefully over the page. "Bart, have you got a pen and ink?"

With the quill and muddy ink the saloonkeeper brought, he entered his grandfather's final date. He turned the book to let Johnson look at it.

"Bart, what do Litt. B. and LL. D. mean?"

"Something about college, ain't it?" Bart asked. "I don't get that Litt. B., but LL. D. is a lawyer, I think. Hell," he grunted, "Harry wasn't no lawyer! He was just the best drinking and fighting man Chito ever had."

"Watch your language," Bill said, pulling his belt up. "You're talking to a lawyer's grandson. He may have been a no-good souse in this town, but he must have been respectable back there in Troy! You see that about my old man being born the same day my grandmother died? She died in childbirth, and the old man was so broke up he took to drink and came West."

Bart poured him another drink. "You're drunk, Billy, but not drunk enough."

"Maybe so, maybe so. But from now on I can look anyone in the eye and know that my family is as good as his. I don't have to be ashamed that my father was a drunk, and the son of a drunk. Why, look here, Bart! Harry brought my dad out West and tried to raise him by himself. What kind of a cull would he make of him? Bad enough, I guess, that my mother ran away from him. That sort of proves my old lady wasn't such a bad sort, either, doesn't it?"

Johnson nodded sourly, a glint of humor in his eyes. "I guess it does."

Bill's hand was clenched about the whiskey glass. "Laugh all you damn' please. It means something to me." Then he looked around to see why the saloon had gone quiet.

Amory had come in to stand there in his frock coat and gray-checked trousers, his chin up, something like Lee at Appomattox. Cheney fell in behind him, and to his right Jarco walked past them to confront Bart Johnson.

"I locked you up last night, Johnson."

Johnson gave Bill an uneasy look. What he saw in his face caused him to straighten up, loop his bar towel over his shoulder, and face it out.

"That's all right for a starter," he said. "What comes next?"

"We lock you up as well as your saloon . . . that comes next!" Jarco retorted.

Then Charlie Amory saw Bill, and advanced. He stopped and placed his hand on the bar, very grave, very erect, a light of righteousness in his bearded face. He spoke in a normal voice — his normal voice, husky and strong — and every man in the Hub listened.

"Why are you doing this, Bill? Why must it be a sword, instead of peace?"

"It's my ancestry," Bill said. "I was born to hang."

"You seem to know how to go about it. Understand this . . . unless you or Johnson can explain why that lock was broken, you are both going to jail, if we have to kill you to take you there."

"We can't go to jail, Senator," Bill objected. "We've got too much to do. There's the election coming up."

Amory peered at him, took two audible breaths through his nose before he said: "What election?"

"City election for marshal and mayor. You'll never guess who's running. Me for marshal and Bart for mayor!"

In the saloon, someone started to laugh and swallowed it as Bill Devlin's head turned. "I mean it . . . we don't like the way this town's being run. We've got a platform worked out."

"Oh, yes?" Amory, back on his heels, was stalling.

Bill reached down and planted the bottle of mescal on the bar. "Our platform is . . . 'We don't leave thumbs in other people's bear traps.' "

Jarco started to look up and bumped into Amory. Amory said coolly: "Get that disgusting relic . . ." He started to sweep it from the bar, but Bill removed it and cradled it in his left arm.

60

"It'll be a pretty liberal administration," he said. "No taxes except for a school and irrigation and the like. You can hire anybody you want to work for you. A man can bounce drunks, even if they've got somebody else's pink ribbon tied around their necks. Think we'll make it?"

"I think," said Charles Amory, "that you're crazy." He turned and retreated to the door. He paused there to say: "You have until tomorrow to close up, Johnson."

The slotted doors went *whup-whup*. There was silence and coolness and a feeling of pressure suddenly released. Johnson leaned both elbows on the bar, propping his head in his hands. "You crazy, damned fool!" he breathed. "Bart Johnson . . . for mayor!"

"What's crazy about that? You'd make a good one. You're too busy to pass laws. You and I have got to run because nobody else in town would have the guts. I decided to stay around here a while, and I can't stay while Amory is running things. The election will be in two weeks. I'm going to ride all over the county talking us up and trying to get people to come in and vote. Providing," he added, "the present administration doesn't resign beforehand."

Johnson looked up curiously, but Bill didn't explain it.

CHAPTER
SEVEN

Bill learned that Amory was staying overnight in Marshal Cheney's room at the jail. That evening he walked down to call on him. Cheney met him in the office. The door to a bedroom was open and Bill could see the foot of a bed and a man lying on it. The marshal placed both hands on the edge of his desk. His eyes, narrow slots of stone, told Bill that he had been crowded about as far as he could be.

"Unless you've come for your permit," Cheney stated, "you'd better back out that door fast."

"I came to see Amory. Is that him?"

"That's him, but you ain't . . ."

"I'll see him, Al," Amory's voice said. The legs moved and rawhide slings creaked as he got off the bed. He came to the door.

Bill said: "It's up to you, but you might prefer Cheney to roll along while we talk."

Amory nodded at the marshal, and Cheney, getting his rifle off the wall, stared at Bill and went out. Bill closed the door. Amory stood silently while Bill arranged a chair so that he could tip back against the wall. It was not coincidence that he commanded a view of the other door and the two windows.

"You're a funny guy, Senator," Bill said.

"I amuse you, do I?" Amory wore no coat or tie and had loosened his collar. The skin of his neck was red and stringy, an old man's skin.

"No, but you're still funny," Bill said. "I might as well let you have it. I found that *Congressional Record* with your secession speech. It was in the cellar up there. Why in hell didn't you send Jarco back after it, when you'd done for Harry?"

Amory sat down behind Cheney's desk. He stared at Bill, slowly and bitterly shaking his head. "It wasn't fair, Bill. I had the best intentions in the world, but those foxes will turn anything a man says."

"Why didn't you stay and fight it out?"

"I told you I got sick."

"Only in the head, Charlie. And you didn't come home to get your health back. You came back to find your self-respect. I guess you were about convinced you'd just dreamed about Washington, weren't you, until Harry came up with the joker? But I still want to know why you didn't go back after it."

Amory's eyes seemed to withdraw. He was entrenching himself behind a wall of denial. "If Jarco went up there, I didn't know it."

"The only way I can figure," Bill said, "is that the stuff was hidden somewhere else before, and Harry moved it later. But he still had to be taken care of, didn't he? It would look bad if he was murdered by one man, so you had him murdered by forty. Who did the dynamiting, Senator?"

"Your grandfather was thought to have done it," Amory said.

"Cut it out!" Bill told him. "We don't have to have a war, but you're forcing us into one. I don't think you'd do the job yourself, but whoever did it for you is as guilty of Harry's death as you are. There's just one way you can clean this up. Get sick again. Go away for your health. I'll take care of the rest of them. But they think you're all-powerful and they'll go to war for you if you say so. As far as I can see, you picked a bunch of box-heads. Except for one thing, they'll stay with you."

Amory gave him a malignant stare. "You want me to leave, eh? So you can fill this town I've built with gambling houses and honky-tonks!"

Bill stood up. "We're on a one-way bridge, Charlie, and I'm going to crowd you right off. I'm going to make asses out of your men and a crook as well as an ass out of you. They'll laugh you out of town when I get through." Then he said: "You know, you and I are a little bit alike. I like to talk, too, and I like people to like me. Every place but here, they have. When we get this straightened out, I think I'll go down to Houston and learn to be a lawyer. We've always had lawyers in my family before. Did you know that? You hung a Yankee lawyer up on Butcherknife Ridge that night."

Amory looked up. His voice took on a strident note. "You're all wrong in your guessing, Bill, but even if you were right . . . what can you do alone?"

"That's the way to talk." Bill chuckled. "Why, I can do this . . . talk a few men into my way of thinking. I don't think there's a man in town who'll stand up to me, as it is. I'm going to prove it by bringing five hundred cows across the river tomorrow. They were stolen from Ellen Hunter, and I made a deal with Mariano Mata to steal them back."

He opened the door. "By the way," he said, "I think I can count on Mariano for some help, too, in case the going gets rough."

The next day was Sunday. Bart Johnson stayed open. Bill had printed a placard on some wrapping paper and fixed it to the backbar behind Jarco's thumb in its glass urn.

Found in Harry Devlin's cellar.
Owner may have same by explaining what
he was doing there.
Vote for Bart Johnson, for a two-thumb mayor!

All conversation revolved about the election. Hidalgo welcomed a change in administration for two reasons. Most of the ranchers, cowboys, and townsmen were tired of Amory's breathing down their necks, and in this country of monotony any kind of excitement was greeted with enthusiasm. Ranch people would carry the word back to their neighbors in the deep, hidden pockets of the Bend. Bill foresaw a landslide if it actually went to an election.

Toward mid-afternoon, Johnson began to worry. He came over to where Bill was shooting snooker pool. He watched Bill drop a red ball and draw a line on a number.

65

Bill missed, and Johnson stood close to him and said: "I don't like all this peace an' quiet. Why don't Amory come down here and make a speech?"

"Maybe they're packing to leave."

"Don't be funny. What if they come after us?"

"You don't know Amory. He doesn't like witnesses. He may back out yet."

"Like hell."

Johnson went back to wash glasses.

By now, Bill was fairly certain of what Amory was waiting for. He had dealt him an ace last night; the only question was whether he possessed the courage to use it. At three o'clock, Bill paid off his pool losses and went over to the bar. "Buy you a drink, Bart," he said.

"Birthday?" Johnson asked. He reached for a bottle of *berrateaga*, which was Mexican for catastrophe under a cork.

"No, Maybe a wake. Hold onto that Bible for me, will you? I'm going to be out of town for a day or two."

He went out, saddled his horse in the corral, and lingered a moment to gaze northwest, across the river. This time of day the sun worked low above the distant red-velvet Carmens, the leaves of the cottonwoods flashed along the river, and the air began to cool, with a fragrance in it of sage and warm earth.

He swung the pony out the gate. He had gone about two miles when he heard a horse behind him. He pulled around and waited. Bart Johnson, his elbows flapping, rode up. Johnson wore his old bone-handled

Peacemaker, the first time it had seen daylight in fifteen years.

"What's up?" Bill asked quickly.

Johnson said: "You never paid me for that drink."

"This is a fine thing," Bill said. "You can't trust a Devlin to pay his liquor bill. Why, that's the only kind of bill we've paid in thirty years. Here's your four-bits and get on back."

Johnson caught the coin. "You're a cagey lad, Bill. But I want to watch you pick up those cattle. Everybody in town's been talking about it. Five's been getting one that you make it."

Bill turned the pony back into the high-center wagon road. "You're old enough to know your mind," he said. "But you may not be around to collect your winnings."

They jogged on until they came to where a large group of riders had come in from the east. The road and the bar pits at each side were pocked with hoof marks. A half hour passed, and then out of the *bosque* of gray willows they came into sight of a low, conical hill a few hundred yards west of the river. This was Sombrero Peak.

They could see a cinnamon cloud of dust rising from behind the hill. They proceeded to the wide, shallow ford, and here Bill saw that a group of riders had crossed recently. Not the Hidalgo men, for the tracks came from the direction of Tascosa Creek. Tom Caslon had kept the date. Still they did not know where the others had gone, but, as Bill turned his pony toward the ford, he heard a great stir of horses in a grove of cottonwoods along the foot of the cliff.

Out of the trees rode Charlie Amory, Cheney, Ostrander, and a dozen men Bill did not know. Jarco, mounted on a sorrel pony hardly larger than a Shetland, was a ludicrous figure. They bore down on the men by the river.

Johnson turned a strained face to Bill. "Too proud to run?"

"It's all right. They know Mata's watching this. They won't try anything until they know how many men he's got with him."

The first thing Bill saw was that Amory was drunk. The velvet touch was gone. He was a red-faced, large-mouthed man who fought his horse down, placing his hand on his hip with the imperious gesture of a cavalry colonel.

"You're a bigger fool than I thought you were," he declared. "I didn't think you were insane enough to try it."

"Why not? Cattle buying isn't against any law I know of."

"Border hopping is," snapped Al Cheney. Cheney was nervous, his eyes dark and his lips pallid, like a barely noticeable scar.

"These cattle are paid for," Bill said.

"They're wet beef, and they aren't coming across," Amory insisted. "Devlin, I'm trying to save you from what we had to do to your grandfather. But if you bring one steer across that river . . ."

"Oh, then it was you that hung him?" Bill remarked quickly and with a lift to his voice.

Amory started. Then he said recklessly: "We don't apologize for anything we've done. Will you go back?"

Bill glanced at the sun. "We'd better get started, Bart. We aren't going to have much time, as it is."

CHAPTER
EIGHT

He put his horse down the shelving sandy bank into the river. Johnson followed him, his face tense. He stayed with Bill as he picked his way across the muddy threads of water in the wide wash. He was breathing stertorously through his nostrils and swearing softly under his breath, unable to forget the guns trained on their backs.

As they went up the far bank, Bill saw Mata waving his great, silver-*concha*ed hat on the slope of the peak. Mata rode down to meet them. Tom Caslon was with him, but the rest of the Squared Circle men were behind the hill with the herd.

Mata's bland, brown face broke into a smile. "Lotsa men over there, Beel. They like you, eh? Want to shake your hand."

"Got my cattle?" Bill asked shortly.

"Only four hundred, Beel. Got my money?"

Dismounting, Bill opened a saddlebag and began to count the money onto the ground. Mata recounted it into his sombrero. "*Hecho*," he said. "Now, how you going to get them across?"

"How do you usually get cattle anywhere? Push 'em." Bill glanced at Tom Caslon, who sat hipshot in his saddle with a wheat-straw cigarette attached to his lower lip. It was impossible to tell whether he was nervous; he always looked unhappy and bothered.

The Mexican began to rub his palms together. "*¡Cáspita!* You let me handle it. I show you."

"I'll handle it," Bill said.

He rode back and had the men start working the cattle into line. Two men rode flank at each side of the column as the animals trotted toward the river. Bill and the rest fell in at the drag, dimly seen figures in the heavy afternoon dust. Across the river, Amory's men were opened out in a long thin line.

Bill told Mariano: "They'll expect us to come in behind the steers, so that's no good. I'm banking that they fire into the herd to keep it from making the bank. If they do, fine. After they get them tangled up, we come around both sides and push Amory's boys together in a sack."

The first of the steers slid down the bank and stopped to drink, but the cowpunchers choused them on. A ragged, brown column with clacking horns, they labored over the sand. Bill began driving them harder, swinging his rope and shouting. The first of the column was not far from the bank. Bill saw Jarco wheel on his undersize pony and break for the trees. He watched, hoping the rest would catch the fever, but the long line with the white-bearded horseman at the center held together.

The steers reached the bank and went up hard, lunging, falling, scrambling to the top. Amory leveled his rifle into the mass and began to fire. Immediately

71

there was confusion, the leaders breaking back and falling under the hoofs of following steers. Still they came, striking up a churning dust on the bank, while Amory's men pumped their lead into the cattle.

Bill let out a yell and fired a single shot in the air. He loped away to the left, drawing the Americans with him. Mata led his crew around the other flank.

Ostrander was the man who saw them coming. At the end of the line, he shouted the warning and wheeled his horse, firing back over his shoulder, as he loped away. Bill fired two shots that missed. Then he heard Caslon's gun pop and saw Ostrander rise in the stirrups to be thrown heavily to the ground.

The Spade men near him wheeled to the center. There was commotion now on the far flank, where Mata's border-hoppers were slashing viciously into the firing line. A Mexican's saddle was emptied. Then two Americans reeled and were lost in the mass of horsemen who rode over them. Mata spurred straight through, looking for Amory.

But Bill's eyes were on Al Cheney, who had dismounted and crouched on one knee with his cheek pressed against the stock of his saddle gun. A chilling sensation struck Bill as if he were looking down the very barrel of the marshal's gun. He saw the pale flash of powder flame and at the same instant felt his horse falter and begin to rear, squealing. Bill quit the saddle and rolled over in the dust, hearing something strike the ground near him and whine off across the river.

He had to scramble away to avoid the threshing pony. A small clump of Spanish bayonet presented itself. Even this shelter seemed blessed. Cheney was a good shot; from his position he could put a bullet where he wanted it. Bill thrust his carbine through the gray-green spikes, rested the star on Cheney's shirt atop the front sight, and slowly took up trigger slack. A pulse pounded in him, seeming to shake his whole body.

The gun recoiled against his shoulder. Dust whipped from the ground a few feet in front of the cactus, so that for a moment Bill could not see the effect on Cheney. Then he saw him lying on his side with his hand clutching the front of his shirt, stirring slowly on the ground.

Something within Bill Devlin began to tremble, something that hated violence. He swore, snapped the shell out of the smoking chamber, threw the bolt back, and got onto his feet.

Mata's men were cutting the others to pieces. Some had tried to ride into the trees and been shot from the saddle. Others had stood their ground, but they were as dead now as the ones who fled. Johnson's horse was buck-jumping and the big saloonkeeper was firing wildly, panicked but still in the fight. Bill started walking toward the small knot of men who had gathered around Amory. He fired as he advanced, stopping to draw a bead, and then walking on as he reloaded. When he saw Amory, he got a shock. The rancher had dropped his gun. He stood with his arms hanging at his sides and his chin high, a martyr's pose. His white hair stirred in the breeze. To the last, he had to justify himself.

Bill had thought he wanted nothing so much as to kill the man who lynched Harry Devlin, but now he knew he could not. It was Mariano Mata, riding at the head of three of his men, who did for the senator. Mata's arm went up, the silver-mounted revolver flashing. It descended. The heavy butt fell like an axe on Amory's head. Amory crumpled, and one of the other Mexicans fired a shot into his face and let his pony run over him.

There was a party at the Hub that night. Up under the shadow of Sombrero Peak they had buried the men who were beyond a doctor's help. The wounded they brought into town. The corks began to pop in Johnson's place, and before they finished Bart Johnson was the drunkest man in his own saloon.

In the morning, Bill Devlin brought a bottle and a glass to the room where Johnson slept. Bart drank shakily and peered at the tall, freshly shaven man who wore polished boots and well-brushed pants and coat. "What are you slicked up for . . . my funeral?"

Bill said offhandedly, but with color in his face: "I may stop by the Hunter place on my way up. Shoot, I'm not really slicked up, just kind of . . ."

"Just kind of duded up like a damned, courtin' fool," said Johnson with disgust. "Marriage! You can try it, but you won't never like it."

"I don't know," Bill said. "I'm a quiet sort of a guy, really. I've got a hunch I may."

Johnson drank out of the bottle, peered closely at him, and said: "I'll be danged if I don't think you are.

74

You're a disappointment to me, Bill. Right from the start you've been a disappointment. But many happy returns, anyway."

BORDER MAN

"Border Man" first appeared in *Dime Western* (1/50) and is remarkable for the ease and skill with which Frank Bonham combines a number of disparate elements and characters into a colorful, suspenseful narrative set in the Arizona-Mexico border country. The tale concerns a prolonged, cattle-killing drought, roving bands of revolutionaries, an unscrupulous cattle buyer, an opportunistic marshal, a vicious ex-revolutionary general turned cattle thief, a cash-poor Mexican *hacendado*, a young woman determined to drive an inherited herd of prime beef from Texas to California, a resourceful small-rancher hero, and a grim fight for survival of both men and cattle in the parched Mexican badlands. Most Western writers would have needed a full-length novel to do justice to the story Bonham tells vividly and concisely in less than 15,000 words.

CHAPTER
ONE

Rowson dipped tepid shaving water from the horse trough and scrubbed up a lather. The mirror hung from a nail in the cement water tank. He stropped the razor and squinted at himself. He was coming to look like the country: brown and drought-bitten. Even his eyes seemed to have faded like old denim. Another few months of it and there would be no southern Arizona and maybe no Page Rowson.

It was mid-afternoon. The leaves of the trees sheltering his rock and adobe ranch house hung limp as hounds' tongues. But lack of breeze was a blessing: wind merely meant dust, not coolness. Most of the heat was burnt out of this day, now that he had spent twelve hours grubbing around back alleys of his place looking for starving cattle. In this tired and windless hush he heard Bat Lyndon and the Mexican, Angel, riding back to the ranch from Frontera. Lyndon was a black-browed, deep-set man of fifty, utterly without humor. Like many humorless men he was pessimistic. Rowson saw him and the Mexican water their horses. He expected no good news from town.

Lyndon was Rowson's ramrod. He lay on the ground and chewed a match. "How would you like to sell a hundred head of cattle to Payson's slaughterhouse for four dollars a head?"

"Is that dressed-out or on the hoof?"

"Gift-wrapped, most likely. Town's still full of railroad travelers. They're sleeping in the livery stables and saloons. And there ain't much chance of them going on to Hermosillo soon, because the Maderistas still got the railroad. So they're eating us out of grub and Payson's slaughtering about four times as much beef as ever."

Rowson flipped peppery lather at the tree. "That the best you could drum up?"

"That's all I could drum up. Except some news. You remember a fella named Larned?"

Rowson pulled him back from memory — a heavy-mannered cattle buyer who had tried to buy a holding ranch here last fall. The world would be a happier place for fewer Vance Larneds, he felt. "I remember him. He offered two-thirds market price for cattle and tried to buy up notes on ranches all over the county. What about him?"

"He's your new neighbor. He was just a piece behind us on the road."

Rowson sat down. "The hell! He's got an eye for trouble like a turkey buzzard. Whose place?"

"Hance's. Old Hance quit."

"Old Rowson would like to quit, too," sighed Page Rowson, who was twenty-seven and an inch below average height. He had a lithe body with hips no wider than his pockets, and slender brown features. "What's he want with a little frying pan like that? He couldn't crowd half his ambition onto the Walking R."

"Just a holding spot. He's still a cattle buyer."

Rowson finished shaving, thinking of Vance Larned. Larned was probably all right; he simply was not Rowson's taste in men. He could not quite mask his eagerness at hearing a fellow mortal was in trouble.

Down the wide and hill-lined pass in which Rowson's Snaketrack Ranch headquartered came the rattle of horse-shoes. Larned and two companions entered the yard. Vance Larned was a tall but hunched man of middle age, lean and hard-fleshed. His face had two hollows under the cheek bones like healed bullet holes. His brows were thorny and his chin was like a smith's sledge. Raising his hand, he grinned at Page. "Still hanging on, eh?"

"Fixing to expand," Rowson said. He looked at the buyer's companions and smiled. "You're in bad company."

Marshal Bob Hamma saw the edge of the joke. He didn't smile. He struck his pommel with the reins ends and glanced about the yard. Sam Shackleford, who occasionally served a paper for the marshal or did an unpleasant job for someone else, was Larned's other companion.

Larned left the saddle. "You knew I'd bought out Charlie Hance? Marshal Hamma's giving me a horseback survey of my land. Sam Shackleford will ramrod it for me."

They shook hands while Bat Lyndon and Angel lay on the ground, inspecting a slow-wheeling buzzard in the sky. The marshal and Shackleford dismounted and patronized the water pipe with its cold, steady stream bubbling into the trough.

Larned spoke in gruff privacy to Rowson, as if they were somehow set apart a bit from these other men who worked for them. "I don't plan to be around a great lot," he said. "This is central for buying, though. I can hold a herd or two here while I wait for railroad cars." Larned's narrow, craggy face pinched. "I suppose you'll be thinning your herd?"

"Why?"

"You can't maintain the same herd in drought times that you can in fat. You'll have to buy feed or sell cattle." Larned spoke rapidly, driving the point in like a wedge.

Rowson rubbed his shiny jaws, still stinging with the soap. "I suppose I'll do like my pappy taught me . . . hang and rattle."

Marshal Hamma suddenly pointed a stubby finger at him. "And there, by God, is what's wrong with this country! Men like you hanging and rattling while they murder the range. If I was making laws for this country, I'd serve papers on you to feed your cattle or sell them. Because when this drought breaks, there ain't going to be any grass to come back."

Rowson regarded him steadily. "What's the split?" he asked.

"Split?"

"How much do you get for rigging men into selling to Mister Larned?"

"That's a damned unneighborly thing to say," Larned snapped.

"But grave robbing's a damned unneighborly thing to do."

The silence was thick. Bat Lyndon's raw, small voice announced thoughtfully: "They can smell 'em."

Everybody looked at him. Still lying on his back, he was peering into the sky.

"Smell what?" asked Shackleford, a sober and obtuse cowboy with an unshaven brown face as dark and greasy as the backside of a flitch of bacon.

"Trouble. They smell carcasses and come two hundred miles to pick the eyes out."

"Oh," Larned said. "Buzzards."

Lyndon sighed — "Yep, buzzards." — and looked at the cattle buyer.

Larned's rawhide face got a little red. Suddenly he turned back to his horse and mounted. Marshal Hamma stood glowering at Rowson and his foreman. He said: "I've heard of fellers talking themselves into trouble with their big mouths, Rowson. Mister Larned come out here in good faith . . . to take some cattle off your hands or even buy you out, clean. Kind of think about what you'll do if this dry holds."

Larned rode close to Page Rowson. "I'm more of a doer than talker," he stated. "I won't come back here and brag that I told you so, but I'll tell you now . . . you're heading for starvation. I make one price for my friends and another for men who don't know how to be friendly. When you send for me next time, you'll know what price to expect."

Rowson looked him over, smiling faintly. "You like this county of ours, don't you? I'll bet you've been having the local paper mailed to you ever since you were here last, reading about the drought. So now the smell's reached you and you've come to pick the eyes."

Shackleford, big and dark-browed, roused like a liver-spotted hound. "You look here . . ." He lumbered toward Page, his long arms stiff at his sides.

Page said: "No. You look. Don't go any further than you really want to." He stood placidly in his spotted cotton shirt and bleached Levi's, his chaps mended with copper wire at the knees. Marks of prosperity were lacking, but self-sufficiency shone on him like the rivets in a new pair of jeans.

Shackleford hesitated, glancing at Vance Larned, and Larned grunted: "Come on." He rode past the mossy cement water tank to the road.

Near sunset Rowson built a fire in the sheet-iron stove and sliced meat from the cooler. A fragrance of chili and *frijoles* reached him through the open window. Angel and his missus, Libertad, were having *refritos*.

Page said to Lyndon: "Let's drop in on Angel. Too hot to cook."

Angel was a small, broad-shouldered man of forty, his chief prides the man he worked for, his mustaches, and his wife. Libertad was not yet thirty, pretty and casual, with a brood of shy, grinning children. The house was dirt-floored but recently sprinkled, clean and cool.

84

The men ate, while Libertad moved from the brick stove to the table on bare feet. "I forgot to tell you," said Bat Lyndon. "Pío Noriega's in town, stalled with the rest of them. Don't know how anxious he'd be to get back, anyhow. They're making jerky out of *hacendados* these days."

"Another one," said Angel, "who only comprehends to hang and rattle. They stole ten thousand cattle from him last year."

Divide it by two for proper proportion, Rowson reflected, and it was still hard lines. Out of this news grew an idea. He asked the Mexican: "Sure about that?"

"My nephew, in Candiles, told me last month. The ranch of *Don* Pío is sick."

Rowson slowly chewed a tortilla and made a thoughtful sound. Libertad moved to the door. "*Caballeros,*" she said.

Page walked outside. They came from the northeast, three horsemen splashing across the thin belt of water between the lacy salt cedars. Rowson watched them, touched by uneasiness. "Go out the back," he said to the others.

He watched them come on. It would not be unthinkable that revolutionaries should raid this far north, which was only ten miles from the Mexican border. But these men sat *gringo* saddles and rode good horses, and they reined in at the water trough and glanced about. Rowson went out.

Spotting him, one of the men left his horse and walked to the hut. He was lean, bearded, and dusty, his eyes pinched. He gave Rowson his hand. "Mott

Rawlings," he said. "My friends and I are heading for Frontera. This the way?"

"Eleven miles. You're welcome to stay overnight."

Rawlings looked uneasily up the shallow valley. "Thanks, brother. We'll move along. Unless . . ." He glanced back at his companions, who were rolling smokes while their horses drank. He asked: "You wouldn't be needing hands? We're looking for work."

"All of you?"

"You don't have to hire us all." Rawlings grinned. "We ain't brothers. We were . . . with a trail herd until just recent."

"Quit?" Page asked shortly.

The cowpuncher's restless eyes sought the northeast again. "Damn' right we quit," he said.

"Then I couldn't use you, anyway. My good luck would be the drover's bad luck . . . until you quit on me when I needed you."

Rawlings looked straight into his face. "Did you ever punch cattle for a woman?"

Surprised, Rowson said: "Why . . . ?"

"Then don't pass judgment on a man that's just finished a hitch working for a female! Once I worked for an old critter that put sticks under our blankets so we'd be glad to get up in the morning. He was a cow-country missionary compared to this one. We ain't tasted beef for two months. We furnished our own horses and nobody in camp could have a bottle and she counted the cups of coffee we drank. This morning we just saddled and rode." He made a brief nod. "Thanks for the water, friend. We'll be moving along."

From the yard, Page watched them string out through the cottonwoods and cross a ridge. Then he began to laugh, and went back to tell the others about it. He and Bat joshed Libertad about her sex being too tough to work for, and it was something less than an hour later that the woman named Abbie Gaines rode hell-for-leather into the Snaketrack yard.

Rowson was sitting in a rawhide chair, tipped back against the front of his shack. Bat was plaiting a hair bridle he had been working on for two years. The girl appeared in the dusty yard with a hard clatter of hoofs, turning her horse broadside before them. The dusk provided the type of light women favored, because it favored them, but Page saw she did not need special favors. Obviously she was shapely, although dressed in a faded blue Army shirt that had been taken in, and in jeans. Her hair was dark and brushed back, pulled into a single, short braid by a yellow ribbon.

"Where are they?" she demanded.

"They rode on. They were looking for work."

"They've got work, as I'll show them when I catch them. Why didn't you hold them for me?"

"Why should I have?"

She thought about that, then dismounted. Rowson, mastering his grin, remained seated. "I'll water my horse," she said, "and be getting on. Isn't there a town near here?"

"Frontera, on the border. You might as well spend the night here . . . that is, with the Sierras, my 'puncher and his family."

"Mexicans?" she asked.

Rowson looked up levelly. "They're good enough for you."

Her hardness was unmasked for a moment. "Oh, I didn't mean . . . well, never mind. I would be obliged for some crackers or something I can carry along."

Rowson went to the horse trough and washed the cracked enamel cup. He filled it and gave it to her. She drank with her eyes closed. "I hear you're taking a herd somewhere." He spoke very quietly.

She filled the cup again. "California."

"Tough season for that. Where you from?"

"You're awful curious, aren't you?"

"Always, with a lady."

"I wasn't sure you knew I was a lady. You didn't get up until you had to." She turned to face the ranch house. "If I could have something . . . tortillas, biscuits . . . ?"

Rowson walked to the shack and brought out a paper bag with some tortillas in it and a can of sardines. "I ask only one thing of my guests. Their names."

"Abigail Gaines. Brownsville, Texas."

"Long way from home, Abbie." Rowson smiled, still holding onto the bag. "Why California?"

"I have a brother-in-law in San Diego County. He has cattle. I'm bringing seven hundred white-faces my father left me."

"I hope you've still got seven hundred when you make it. There's no graze beyond Gila Bend. Nothing but sand. No water."

"You could almost say that of Frontera." She faced the sunset-tinged ridge beyond the trees. "I take that trail, then?"

"I wish you'd stay, Abbie. You aren't going to take those men back with you, anyway."

"Then I'll hire others."

"Not to cross the Gila and Colorado deserts. People from the Colorado come here to get cool. They sit around with shawls over their shoulders, and it ain't really chilly here."

She stubbornly kept her eyes from him, but he saw her chin weaken a little. "Oh, I'll make it. If I can get men."

"You won't. There's one thing you could do, though."

He shook dry tobacco flakes onto a paper. He made her ask it: "What's that, mister . . . ? You haven't told me your name."

"Rowson. Why, you could lease pasturage from me. Temporary basis, that is. There's a cattle buyer in town. You might even make a dicker with him. But don't try to take these cattle across the Colorado deserts."

She sniffed. Her features were fine, not quite haughty, but held self-respect. Her lower lip was deep and rich, and her eyes were as lustrous as a Mexican girl's. "I shouldn't say you had any more graze than you needed for yourself."

"But I'm bringing in feed from Mexico. The rains will hit one of these days. Until they do, I'll artificially feed my cows. I've dodged it too long. Tomorrow I'm going in to make a bargain for hay and grain."

"They'll rob you." She declaimed it as though she knew merchants to the cores of their black hearts.

"Not this man. He's in a spot, too." He lighted the cigarette, dropped the match, and let the smoke gather between them. "I won't rob you. You'll pay just what the cattle eat."

"But what do you make out of it?"

"Maybe some calves. You come with seven hundred, you leave with seven hundred."

She put out her hand suddenly. "That's a bargain, then." She smiled. Her relief was a softness in her features. "I . . . I'll ride back and tell my men . . . I still have two . . . to hold the cattle there tonight."

"No need. I'll send Angel. My foreman will bunk with me and you can have his room."

Afterward he wondered why he had done it. She was trouble in a saddle, but he could not see her riding on, perhaps to her death. Or was it involved with a desire to discover whether she was as self-sufficient as she thought she was?

There was an affinity between towns and men, it seemed to Rowson, and Frontera was his kind of town. Straddling the border of northern Sonora, it took its tempo and good nature from the *vaqueros* to the south. Venders sold pumpkin seeds and *piloncillos* of brown sugar, black cigarettes, and gaudy serapes. Mexican and white children played in the streets and you couldn't tell an American cowboy from a Mexican until he opened his mouth. Their skins were burned brown and they wore taut leather leggings for the most part and collarless cotton shirts, their hats the shape of cones of sugar.

Abbie Gaines shopped. She beat old Morrison down on prices until Page was ashamed to carry the packages out. As he packed the provisions in the spring wagon, she spotted Mott Rawlings, one of the three men who had deserted her the day before. Dressed in a gown with a wide, gray skirt and tight bodice, which imparted to her somewhat the shape of a hand bell, she swept across the street and cornered him against a building.

Frontera slowed while she roasted the cowpuncher. He must have made some half-hearted offer to return. The last thing Rowson heard was her declaration: "Why, I wouldn't have you with a dowry of ten registered herd bulls! Deserting a cowman in a tight! Find some place where they run sheep, Rawlings. That would be the work for you."

A man near Page breathed: "*¡Qué chata!* I would not be penned with her for all the bulls in Sonora!"

It was the voice of a lithe Mexican in business clothing, only his cowman's hat typifying him as a rancher.

Rowson said: "The warm-blooded ones make for fun, *Don* Pío."

Don Pío Noriega looked around, came forward with an exclamation, and took Rowson's hand. "Not the blood that boils over, my friend. If you are acquainted with her, it will be your misfortune."

He was laughing, a cleanly built, Indian-dark man of forty years. Rowson saw Abbie returning to the wagon. "She's leasing pasturage from me. Will you have something to eat with us at the railroad café? Something I'd like to ask you."

Noriega glanced at the girl, her dark hair glistening in the sun, and said: "I take that chance."

Abbie worried Page by putting a look of stark suspicion on the Mexican as soon as they were seated around a dirty table in the restaurant. Noriega's co-operation could spell defeat or survival. Noriega had the grass and grain that might save Rowson. His cattle ranch covered a fifth of the state of Sonora.

"Are you one of those revolutionaries?" the girl demanded.

Noriega touched his heart in pain. "*Señorita*, I am one of those shirtless *hacendados*. They take ten thousand of my cattle last year. They steal my corn. They leave me half a million acres of range, and hardly the cattle to feed my village."

Abbie said: "Oh, forgive me. Then you're our friend . . . not a spy at all. I have heard . . ." She shook her head over what she had heard.

Rowson commiserated with the rancher. "And to top it all, you're marooned here, eh? Coming back from El Paso?"

"*Sí*. I went to buy cattle. But *pesos* are cheap. The cattle I could buy I would not bother to ship."

Page rolled a cigarette. "Looking for white-faces?"

"I had hoped for white-faces, stock I can sell for dollars instead of *pesos*."

Rowson said: "I need hay. You need cattle." He lighted a cigarette.

The Mexican frowned slightly, then leaned on his elbows. "Does something occur to you, *Don* Page?"

"Something occurred to me last night, when I heard you were in town. If I could cut hay on your mountain meadows, I'd pay for it with good herd animals. I've got to thin mine anyway. I can't support the number I'm carrying. Your range has been resting."

Noriega took Rowson's large, rough hand in his own lean, brown one. "Now we are talking like *compadres*. I will not rob you on the hay. And there is grain and corn going to the weevils."

Abbie Gaines came in quietly: "If you could pay cash for other cattle, *Don* Pío, I have seven hundred white-faces."

"My life's blood I would give you, but I cannot give cash."

"Cash or nothing," said Abbie. She shrugged, and looked away. *Bone hard*, thought Rowson. *Bone hard*.

Noriega tapped on the dirty cloth. "These cattle I will take into the mountains. Until the trouble ends. It is now rumor that an army is coming from Chihuahua City to clean out Sonora. Then I am in business again. When do you wish the hay?"

"Now. Come out today and we'll start the cut in the morning."

Three men entered the café, standing near the entrance to seek a table in the crowded room. They were Marshal Hamma, Sam Shackleford, and a Mexican. Rowson didn't hear Noriega rise. But suddenly he saw the rancher moving across the sheet-metal floor with his glass of wine in his hand, making for the trio. He saw this other Mexican — a slack-bellied man in a tight, black coat and brown chaps, two guns belted on — recognize Noriega and throw his hand before his face. But the wine had slipped out of the tumbler and struck him in the eyes.

Hamma was bawling. "Get back, spik! Manteca, I'll handle it!"

Noriega was spitting Spanish imprecations at the gross-bellied man. Hamma, his fist knotted, was moving in behind the rancher. Rowson picked up an empty coffee cup and fired it at the marshal. It struck him heavily in the shoulder. Hamma pivoted, pulling at his gun, but Page's was already in his hand and he was saying: "Outside might be the place to settle this, Marshal."

Hamma hesitated.

Rowson said to the girl — "Sit tight." — and rose to put a hand on Pío Noriega's shoulder. "What's the matter? Who is he?"

The Spanish language was framed for irony. Rigid under Rowson's hand, the Mexican said: "Speak softly, *amigo*. We are in the company of a general . . . Manuel Manteca, so called, late of the revolutionary army. If their pelts were longer, we would call it a pack. This is General Manuel Manteca, who slaughtered what he could not steal of my herds, and sold what the army could not eat. Until he became too filthy for the army."

Manteca, the stain of the liquor spreading over his shirt as it trickled from his face, was white with anger. His features were broad and aggressive. His lips were wide and flat, as though they had been turned back. He glanced at Page. "Your friend is insane. I am a dealer in cattle."

Rowson smiled at Hamma. "He'd have a permit, wouldn't he?"

Hamma growled and thrust Noriega through the door. "We'll talk about cards later."

In the sun before the adobe station wall, Hamma put Noriega's back to the hot bricks. The *hacendado* had accepted his error. He answered the marshal's questions quietly. "I say that it is true. I retract nothing. If Manteca is in town, lock up your money and your women."

Manteca waved a large hand. "The heat. It makes mad dogs of sane men."

Noriega's eyes were dark and gritty. "Greed does the same, eh?" He confronted Rowson. "*Mas tarde, amigo.* I go to my hotel to arrange my valise."

Hamma's warning followed him: "Be throwing wine on another man and I'll set you loose in the desert."

They stood there. Manteca grumbled as he wiped wine from his face and neck. Rowson turned to go back, but saw Abbie Gaines in the restaurant doorway.

Shackleford was speaking to him. "This fella was looking for you."

Rowson frowned at the Mexican. "You've found me."

Out of anger and confusion, Manteca tried to assemble the ingredients of good nature. He smoothed his shirt over his belly, smiling. "You raise cattle, no? I buy cattle. I can sell all the good *gringo* cattle I can take to Hermosillo. It occurred to me . . ."

"No," Rowson said.

Manteca shrugged. "Be foolish, my friend. I pay twenty dollars a head."

Rowson turned back. "Twenty dollars?"

Manteca's fat smile came. "Not *pesos*. Noriega lied . . . I am not general, I am revolutionary impresario. I buy cattle for the armies. I take all you sell me, pay earnest money, and bring back the rest of the cash when I return."

Rowson began to laugh. "Show me the shell-and-pea game next time, General. I'm not so foolish on this one."

Abbie was saying: "Twenty dollars, Mister Manteca? I have some cattle I'll sell." Rowson took her arm, but let his hand fall away when she faced him hotly. "I can manage my affairs, Mister Rowson!"

Shackleford gave her a sober smile. "You won't go wrong, miss. Vance Larned is selling cattle to Manteca, and if Larned says he's all right . . ."

The girl looked into Manteca's face. "I'd want twenty-two dollars, however, if it's part credit."

Manteca inclined his head. "Agreed. The cattle . . ."

". . . are on Mister Rowson's land just now. If you can come out to look them over, we can talk about the details."

Manteca shook her hand. "*Su servidor, señorita. ¿Caballeros?*" The men went inside the restaurant and took a table.

Rowson's stare was raw with disdain. "I thought you set store on being a businessman. Do you think you'll ever get the rest of that money?"

"I am quite sure of it," Abbie said.

Rowson looked at her. Hard-headed? Hard like the cold-jawed bronc', he reflected, that ran into a barn to show him it could not be jackassed around. He said: "Well, they're your cattle."

He visited Noriega at the hotel. The Mexican had changed his mind. He would be out in the morning to pick his cattle.

"Keep out of Manteca's way," Rowson said.

"When it is time, I will put myself in his way."

Page pigeon-holed the rest of his town tasks and in early dusk, whistling, went back to the wagon. It was parked under a cottonwood beside a Mexican *cantina*. He had left a boy to watch it. The boy accepted the coin he tossed him but said: "*Señor*, those *hombres*, under the trees there . . ."

The men came from behind the trees, Vance Larned, Bob Hamma, and Larned's ramrod, big Sam Shackleford. They were sober and purposeful. Rowson waited, one hand on the tailgate of the wagon. "Where's your friend?" Rowson asked. "Out selling somebody else a gold brick?"

"You don't trust men much, do you?" Larned asked. His knotty, raw features were sour. "I know Manteca and he's honest. It isn't your place to boycott him."

"He's a pig, a cow-thieving pig," Rowson said pleasantly.

Bob Hamma's blond mustache looked bleached against his ruddy features. "I could say the same about your pard, Noriega. I don't know what you and he were talking about, but if it has anything to do with moving cattle across the border . . ."

Rowson listened.

"Well, does it?"

"If it does, nothing a rusty badge can say will change my mind."

Hamma's temper surfaced. "Then maybe this will!" He stepped in close and held the cowman by the arm. "Move one cow across the line without a permit and you'll forfeit it. Try it again, and . . ."

Rowson's hand took his cigarette to his lips. Then it slashed back, striking the marshal in the mouth. Hamma dodged back, and Rowson said: "Throw your weight around with *pulque* drunks all you like. But don't make me watch any more of it."

Larned and Shackleford were both talking loud and fast, but Page's attention focused down on the marshal. Hamma's hand was at his Colt. Rowson kicked him in the shin and grabbed at his gun hand. He tore it away from the bone-handled Frontier model .45. Hamma ducked his head and butted Rowson on the nose. Catching him by the shirt, Page slugged him heavily in the face. He seized the marshal's gun and threw it under the wagon.

Hamma was a large, dogged man of intemperate angers. He made a strange, wild grimace as he rocked back, slugging with both fists. Rowson backed up. Something caught his spur and he tripped. As he went down, he saw Vance Larned moving away. An advantage must be mean before Bob Hamma would pass it up: he came in savagely and raised one foot to stamp at Rowson's face. His spur glittered. Rowson hunched against the wagon wheel and the boot thudded beside his ear.

He scooped a handful of dirt and hurled it upward. Hamma ducked the grit that sought his eyes. In the instant's reprieve, Page Rowson lunged up, driving headlong into him. Hamma tried to hold on. Rowson's knee hurled him back. Silently savage, Rowson hammered at the man's head with a long blow, saw the blood start from the marshal's nose, and moved in while Hamma was still blinded by pain and tears.

Bob Hamma's fists fumbled at him. He tried to retreat, but the rancher went with him, driving short, hard blows into his body. Hamma hunched, loosened by a blow to the belly. Page hauled one in from the side, feeling the good crack of his fist against Hamma's ear. He came erect, breathing quickly and shallowly as the marshal went down and floundered to his knees, sinking back after a moment to lie on his belly with his cheek against the dirt.

Larned's voice came crisply: "Men that make their own laws, Rowson, sometimes get themselves repealed."

Rowson faced him, his anger trembling behind his lips, but holding himself steadily. "That's what happened to Hamma. He's got no more jurisdiction over border traffic than I have."

Larned regarded him gravely. "We've made a bad start, Rowson. I wish we could forget this, and what happened the other day. We'll be living pretty close together to be forever scattering loco weed in each other's pastures."

"I'm a pretty friendly man. But if you come simpering around with any more bootlicking lawmen, you and I will tangle quicker than you can bribe a cow-town marshal."

CHAPTER
TWO

Traveling slowly through the early night, Rowson and the girl drove back to the Snaketrack. The darkness closed them in. Night sounds came eerily. Abbie Gaines, making no point of it, settled herself a little closer to him on the wagon seat as they clattered along the shadow-rotted base of a rim-rock cliff. Rowson observed it with inner pleasure. He began to glance now and then behind them on the road. He peered upward at the shelving cliffs and laid his single-shot, trapdoor Springfield on his lap, humming quietly.

Abbie asked: "I don't suppose he'd be so angry he'd send anyone after you?"

"Hamma? More likely than to come after me himself."

Something swooped low with a stiff rush of feathers. She caught his arm.

"Nighthawk," he said. After a while, he asked: "Whatever possessed you to take the trail alone with those cows, Abbie?"

"I've tried to get used to being alone since my father died. I didn't like trying to ranch alone, so I sold the land and started out with the cattle."

"Not afraid of things, are you?"

"What things?" She moved away stiffly.

"Of being cheated, for instance. Or of seeming to be afraid."

"All I'm afraid of," sniffed Abbie, "is what would happen if I ever trusted anyone as far as he asked me to." They rattled on a while. "You're awfully sure of yourself, aren't you?" she said. "Whipping marshals seems very unwise."

"Myself is all I'm sure of. That, and the fact that you can't trust some Mexicans, such as Manuel Manteca."

"When I need advice," Abbie said, "I'll let you know."

Pío Noriega rode out the following day on a rented horse, glad to be quit of the traffic-glutted town. He and Page arrived at a bargain. With Bat Lyndon, they started a day herd of cattle that would presently be moved southward to the Mexican's ranch in Sonora. It was while they were among the dry sage hills that Manuel Manteca and Vance Larned visited the Snaketrack and conferred with Abbie Gaines. Rowson found this out when he returned that night. He learned it from Jay McQuilty, the girl's foreman

McQuilty was an east Texan with a slow manner of speaking, a leathery cowboy who wore a collar-band shirt with no collar, and batwing chaps twice as wide as he was. His teeth were worn lopsided by his pipe. He had a long, sad, red face with loose-lidded eyes like a hound's. In the bunkhouse where Libertad was arranging a cot for Noriega, he said bitterly: "I reckon I'm shut of them god-damned cows at last. Sick of looking at the same old behinds for a thousand miles. Manteca's taking the whole herd."

"When?" Noriega shot at him.

"Four, five days. He's taking a regular god-damned trail herd down. Three fellers in Frontera are selling to him, too. Same deal. Down payment, the rest in a month."

"*Tontos, puros tontos,*" Noriega breathed.

McQuilty shrugged. "Why? He's paying them the same money down that Larned offers full price. If they get any more, it'll just be a nice surprise."

Rowson tromped out his cigarette. "Four dollars a head! That's not even a down payment. Larned's stampeding them into Manteca's hands. The deal stinks!"

His and McQuilty's glances met, the same thought reaching both. "You'd think," the Texan said, "they'd be bidding against each other, instead of riding around like saddle pards."

"You would," Rowson agreed. "You can't talk her out of it, eh?"

McQuilty's long face writhed into a grin. "Did you ever talk a female into anything? Not one like this, mister. She rode her turns like any of us, all the way across. You'd forget she was a lady, only that she didn't cuss so much."

Pío Noriega thoughtfully pulled on a *papel orozuz* cigarette. "One thing I do not forget . . . that Manuel Manteca was discharged by even that pack of shirtless rebels called an army for cheating. If he is dealing in cattle, it is for himself. Your friend Larned, perhaps, is playing into Manteca's hands."

"A man with an eye as cold as his," Page declared, "never played into anybody's hands. If anybody's being taken, it's Manteca."

Abbie woke Rowson the next morning by clattering utensils in the dishpan. He dressed, and came into the large center room and saw her industriously pumping water into a tea-kettle. Dishes and pans were piled high. She wore the shirt and Levi's again and had her hair pinned up.

"Am I late for breakfast or early for lunch?" Page asked.

Abbie thumped the teakettle on the stove. "I wouldn't eat out of these filthy things without scouring them."

Later, Abbie came out of the cabin as Rowson adjusted a saddle blanket on his gray gelding. He and Noriega were starting the cut immediately. Whistling, he lifted the saddle onto the horse and groped for the cinch.

Abbie said curtly: "I might ride along and see what your country looks like."

"Suit yourself."

He watched her face as she saddled — the contours of her cheek bones gentle and her lips full, her eyes sober and gray, and somehow sad. He appraised the slender figure warmly until she caught him at it and disciplined him with a frown. With Pío Noriega, they rode eastward through the hills, pyramidal as ant hills, scant with warped trees, and beaten cruelly by the heat and drought.

Noriega had an eye for white-faces. Rowson was on his guard not to be dickered out of the best of his bulls and heifers. He steered the Mexican away from where his best stock grazed. He had a bunch of his best cows spotted on a murky thread of green water called Cibola Creek. He had in mind avoiding this area, but, as they rode around the base of some low hills, he heard a sound of cattle running, a cowboy's sharp — "Ho!" — and he pulled the gelding in sharply and listened.

Cibola Creek picked up the water of several springs and crawled down a cañon beyond a low ridge. Rowson asked the girl quickly: "Did you pasture any stock over yonder?"

"No. We rode by yesterday with Manteca. They're farther west."

Rowson said: "Wait here, then." He nodded to Noriega to follow him and started up the slope. When he reached the top, he discovered Abbie following them. Hotly he turned to send her back, but at that instant a horse made a brief, hard run just below them, and a steer thudded against the ground.

Rowson looked into the bottom of the cañon. Boulders studded it, but there were areas of grass and a stone corral within sight. Eight or ten white-faces were penned in the corral. A pair of cowpunchers were branding here, and two more were working over the steer which had just been spilled. They worked hard and earnestly, so earnestly that Rowson had the .45-70 Springfield at his shoulder before one of them saw him.

"¡*Vámonos!*" It was a high, lingering yell. Rowson's gun crashed, and one of the horses went down.

Abbie was on her feet now, running up with a light saddle gun in her hands. Rowson glimpsed her, and turned back. He picked up a rock and threw it at her. She gasped, and ducked behind a rock. Noriega pulled his horse behind a dead cedar that was like a clutch of greasewood roots. He fired a shot from there.

Movement flowed from northwest, down the cañon, the cowpunchers swinging into saddle as they ran beside their ponies. They were dark-skinned, sombreroed men in tight, leather chaps. Rowson remembered — "*We rode by with Manteca . . . .*" Manteca had made mental notes and come back. Rowson bit the end off a paper shell, inserted it, and capped the nipple. His sights hounded a hunched rider for fifty feet; he fired. This man threw his hands aloft, and the pony bucked him into the brush. Noriega fired again, and Abbie came wriggling through the rocks and her gun went off so close to Rowson that his ears rang. He shouted a furious order, but she calmly levered another cartridge into the Spencer rifle she carried.

Between them a slug walloped the ground and mingled dust with the greasy smoke of Rowson's old black-powder cartridges. Abbie rocked with the recoil of her rifle. Rowson stared at her face; she was white as tallow. But she lay there in the rocks as stubbornly as a foot soldier.

A last echo of shod hoofs whispered through the smoke and dust of the cañon floor. The cattle bawled and one of the animals in the corral jumped the fence but hung up on it for a moment.

Presently the three rode down the cañon.

CHAPTER
THREE

The dead Mexican was a small man with a wispy, black chin beard, a border *paisano* in dirty, white pants and shirt. He lay across his gun, a long, homemade musket with a side-hammer. You could not distinguish this man from a hundred others living in Frontera or Old Frontera across the line.

"Manteca's man?" Rowson asked.

Noriega moved him with his foot. "*¿Quién sabe?*"

He walked to the yearling steer tied nearby. The brand, half finished, was a cursive design like an anchor. Noriega shrugged. "Who knows? It is nothing I have seen."

Rowson hadn't seen it, either. He climbed the hill and found Abbie, wiping dirt from her face with a handkerchief.

"The next time you go riding with me," he said, "you go without a gun. You ran a risk of having that pretty face shot off."

"They started it, didn't they?" She had her color back, but her lips looked stiff. "I meant what I said about advice, you know."

Rowson stood there as she rose from her knees. Then he turned in unaccustomed ill nature to his pony. He didn't welcome this agitation he felt over her. She was a termagant, a shrew, and he could imagine nothing worse than to fall in love with such a woman.

"Here's one more piece of advice," he said roughly. "Get out as soon as you can. Because you won't last long in this country."

Noriega came up. Rowson reined in beside him. "Will you take the girl with you? I'll cut back past the house and look around south. There's some stuff in my Ojo Claro pasture I want to bring in."

At the cabin he put jerky and hardtack into a sugar sack. He selected his traveling horse, a leggy dun, changed saddles, and turned the gray into the trap. He left instructions with Angel. Then he rode southwest through the tawny desert hills toward Hance's ranch.

Not over two miles from the ranch he cut the sign of three horses. The prints were still sharp in the hot earth of early evening. He knew the layout of Hance's place. A bald, lavender hill soared a few hundred yards below an unplastered adobe box and a couple of corrals of ocotillo wands. Quartering around, he left his horse in a copse of trees by the tepid stream and climbed the hill. From here presently he found the riders. They were some distance from Larned's cabin, swapping horses in a distant corner of the cattle buyer's main pasture. He watched them finish saddling, leave their own mounts, and cut through a Missouri gate to jog due south.

Night crested along the eastern rim of the hills, darkness invaded the range, and down below a lamp burned. Rowson rode into the ranch yard. He smelled potatoes and meat frying. A man called gruffly: "Who is it?" It was Sam Shackleford's voice.

"Rowson. Larned here?"

"What do you want?" Vance Larned appeared in the doorway, lanky and big-jointed, wearing boots, Levi's, and undershirt. He held a potato in one hand and a butcher knife in the other.

Rowson dismounted and walked to the door. Inside, he saw Shackleford looming like a surly bear behind his trainer, huge and shaggy and suspicious. "You've just lost three horses," Rowson said.

Larned's head bent forward a bit, then he came out, spearing the potato on the knife. "How?"

"Well, you've swapped. Three border hoppers just made you a trade."

Larned turned quickly. "Sam! Saddle your bronc' and bring mine in."

Shackleford bounced massively out the door, but Rowson halted him. "What for? They're clean across the border by now. That's the thing about living with your back door opening on Mexico."

Larned studied him ill-naturedly. "Who were they?"

"That's what I rode over to ask you. Who are they?"

Shackleford roused stiffly. "Rowson, if this is another caper like in town . . ."

"Be quiet," Rowson drawled. "This is for you, Larned. I was hoping to see you pay them off. Seeing them swap horses with you is almost as good, but would it sound as good to a stuffed-elk of a marshal like Bob Hamma? If you're here to buy cattle, I'm here for my nerves."

110

Larned cocked a foot onto the stoop. "I wonder how Arizona ever got along without you to worry about it. What have I done now?"

"I'll tell you what some other men have done. Blot-branded a dozen of my cows. But they were sloppy. I caught them at it. I killed one . . . a Mexican. The ones I missed are the ones who are riding your horses now. They seemed to feel safe about switching."

"You're coming close," Larned remarked, "to talking yourself into trouble."

"I'm coming closer than that to calling you a liar and a cow thief."

Larned's hand brushed from his knee, kinked up by the stoop, to hang at his side. He wore a Wells Fargo Colt in a basket-woven holster. His hand twitched but made no rash move. When Rowson was sure of him, he said: "You run too muddy for me to know what you're up to. But it isn't ranching, and it isn't cattle buying. I'd say it had something to do with Manuel Manteca. If I find either of you on my land, I'll know you've come to fight. *¿Claro?*"

"Get out," Larned said.

Rowson smiled. "I didn't come to stay. I will say I'm glad the light's poor. I'd guess if you ever nerved yourself up to killing, your man would never know what hit him."

He retreated unhurriedly, without losing sight of Larned and Shackleford. He mounted and swung, watched them a moment, and rode into the hackberries.

He arrived at the ranch long after dark. Noriega and the others were abed. The cabin was dark but, as he entered, the ash door of the stove grated open and the ruddy light revealed the room and the person beside the stove. Light glinted on bright steel. The gun quickly came down and the butt touched the floor as Rowson was recognized.

"Well, have you cleaned up the revolutionaries?" Abbie put amused irony into her voice.

Rowson let himself into a rawhide-bottomed chair. He pulled off his boots and wiggled his toes. She came from the stove, trailing the gun. "I'm tired," he said. "Too tired to be badgered."

She turned after a moment and lifted a pot of coffee from the back of the stove. She poured him a cup. She brought a pan of *frijoles* and beef from the stove, served them on a thick china plate, and said: "These are ruined."

He ate hungrily. "I'll have to train Bat to do these tricks." She sat down, a pale, tense presence near him. "There's nothing to keep you up," he said, "if this is all you were waiting for."

"It's not. I just wanted to tell you. Manteca has his herd ready. We leave day after tomorrow."

Rowson laid the fork down. "We?"

She smiled. "You said I'd be cheated. You didn't know me, Page. I'll get my down payment and go along with him to collect the rest. They won't cheat me."

Rowson set the food aside. "You could have let me finish before you took my appetite away. Didn't your mother tell you about white women sashaying around Mexico alone?"

"Yes, but she didn't know about Winchesters."

Lunging up, he went to grip her shoulder. "A woman's got a right to be crazy, or to be pretty, but she's got no right being both. Why is it any of my business if you want to get yourself sworn into the Mexican rebel army?"

"It isn't." She tugged, but his fingers retained her shoulder.

Rowson pulled her to her feet. "Abbie, you aren't going."

Her face was close to his, pallid and stiff. "But I am. It isn't as though I had any other choice. I could stay here, I suppose, and have my cows get ga'nter every day, and pay wages, and not have the increase. But I can sell for decent money right now and go on to California."

It was a moth attack in the face of logic, but a woman could release such moths forever, and a man got worn down fending them off. Rowson's mouth tightened and he brought his palm in a half slap against her cheek. "Crazy," he said. "Both of us. I was crazy to let you stay. You're crazy to go. Slap me for this, Abbie, but don't forget I'll be paying for it."

His arms captured her taut slenderness, crushing her breasts against him. His face pressed against her throat and he clutched a handful of shining dark hair as he kissed the tender skin. She trembled, quieting as his lips moved up to her mouth. But when his arms unlocked, she pulled away, crying.

"You've got no right! Treating me . . . as though . . ."

"Treating you as though I loved you," Rowson said bitterly. "Go to bed, and dream about being a rich woman and having a hundred cowpunchers, but don't forget the part about being lonely."

Rowson and the others — Pío Noriega, Bat Lyndon, and Angel — spent a last day readying the herd for Mexico. A trail brand was scorched into the reddish hides of the two hundred animals. They were bunched on Bullet Creek and left with two cowpunchers, while the others rode back at sundown to pack food and bedrolls into the bug wagon.

Abbie came from her room as they were sitting down to dinner. She wore the Levi's and old Army shirt again, and carried her blankets over her shoulder like a man. She was the essence of self-sufficiency, but Rowson saw through her.

"I'd like to pay you for the pasturage," she said.

"Forget it. I thought you were leaving tomorrow morning, though."

"We are. McQuilty and Manteca's men moved my herd over to Red's Cañon today. We'll leave from there in the morning." She offered her hand. "I hope I haven't upset things too much?"

"Oh, no." Rowson shook hands soberly.

She was waiting for him to say something, and, when he did not, a shadow entered her face. "I hope the rains come soon. Good luck, Page. Always, good luck."

"Good luck to you. You taking any blackberry brandy?"

"What for?"

"For the stomach complaint. You can't set foot in Mexico without picking it up. And sprinkle a little baking powder in your blankets at night and you may keep out the lice. Fifty-fifty chance."

Her lips firmed. "Trailing cattle isn't a luxury even in this country, you know."

"That's right. Well, just keep an eye on Manteca and you may get the best of him. Who all's going?"

"Just McQuilty and Manteca and Larned, I suppose, and a few cowpunchers. You don't need to worry about me. I took care of myself all the way from Brownsville without your advice."

Rowson smiled. "Sure you did. *¡Adiós!*"

She moved to the doorway. "When . . . when do you plan to leave?"

"Tomorrow. But we'll be trailing considerably east of you. The range won't stand two herds on one trail. *Adiós*, Abbie."

Noriega pronounced solemnly: "*Vaya con Dios, señorita.*"

Abbie lifted her chin and departed.

Noriega chuckled. "You attempt to frighten the señorita?"

"She's frightened already. But mostly she's frightened of our knowing it." He ate silently for a while. "Manteca as bad as you said, or is it partly that you happen to hate him?"

"I happen to hate him because he is as bad as I said. If the rebels will not associate with a man, he is unfit for hanging. *Adiós*." He sighed. "That one so pretty should die so young!"

Rowson's fork halted. "Hell, he wouldn't kill her . . ."

"I am thinking more likely that the *señorita* may prefer it. The cattle traffic is not all that Manteca comprehends."

Rowson overslept, awaking to see the rust-stained face of the clock indicating seven o'clock. He was not a man to oversleep, and looked about for a cause. Beyond the window he found it: the sky was scaled with gray clouds.

He dressed hurriedly, feeling vindicated. The rains would come, as they had always come, as he had told them they would when cattlemen argued with him that the border was finished. But it was scant satisfaction that the day was already well begun, that Abbie Gaines's cattle might already have crossed the line into Mexico.

The others came from the bunkhouse, and Bat Lyndon emerged from the room Abbie had relinquished last night. "Never closed my eyes," he said. "Kep' smelling perfume."

Odors of *huevos rancheros* and pans of biscuits filled the Mexican's shack when they went over. Breakfast was gloomy, contrasting with the ordinary trail-drive morning. In the yard the wagon was loaded and hitched with a span of mules. The sun filtered weakly through the clouds. There would be a day or two of clouds, and then — God willing — a pelting thunder-storm.

Rowson thought about this. He saw the grass strengthening, the streams rising, and it left him unmoved. What his mind hoarded was an album of pictures of Abbie. Sitting her horse arrogantly that first day, as she demanded word of her mutineers. Abbie at the stove, slender and dark-haired as she drew loaves of rizzar bread from the oven. Abbie moving closer to him as they drove along the dark road through the hills. His throat tightened. He pushed back his chair.

"Turn them onto the grass again for a couple of days," he said. "I'm going out."

"Where at?" demanded Lyndon, his heavy brows hunching.

"Where the heart goes," said Noriega, "the man follows."

Rowson scowled. "I don't know about that, but I got a notion I ought to be keeping an eye on Vance Larned."

Angel moved his chair back, smoothing his ram's horn mustaches as he rose. "I know the country well, *patrón*."

Rowson glowered. "So do I. You stay here. Keep an eye on that day herd. I'll be back *mañana*."

But when he had ridden a mile and a half, he heard them roaring up behind him — Angel and Noriega and Bat.

CHAPTER
FOUR

The range was like crumpled brown velvet. Over it the sky was gray and ragged, torn by a west wind from the Gulf. There would be rain, there would be grass, but all the profit of it would be months from now. Sloughing off to the south, the range was cut by deep barrancas and low, eroded rims. From one of these they could see, distantly, a dun-colored cloud under the heavy belly of the sky. Cows were moving deeply into Sonora, trailing out of Red's Cañon. Rowson had his line, and now he angled over to the cañon itself. The red walls of it were fluted, gashed by old floods. Cattle sign sprinkled the gravelly earth. They bored through the easy loops of it, not forcing the horses but keeping them on the spur. Noriega, lean and dark, rode at Page's side. They stopped to blow their horses, once, and Rowson sat rolling a smoke.

Noriega said: "To worry is no damn' good, *amigo*."

"To start too late is no damn' good, either."

They were sitting there when Angel raised his hand. "Leesten!"

Blunt iron scraped the earth. Horses were moving toward them. Rowson's eyes rummaged down the cañon; a barranca slashed in a few dozen rods ahead.

He signaled the men. They rode into the winding cleft; he left his horse and walked back. He wedged himself into a fault in the bank. The riders scuffed by him. They were Vance Larned and Sam Shackleford.

"He don't have to take them clean to Mexico City," Shackleford groused.

Larned said: "There's a little matter of an international boundary. Hamma will stick his neck out just so far."

They were gone, then, in a soft fog of dust. So Bob Hamma was in it, for sure. Rowson strode back to his horse. They waited a suitable interval before proceeding down the cañon.

"Who was it?" Lyndon demanded.

Rowson told them. "Something's up. Manteca isn't playing this alone."

The cañon debouched onto a broad plain. Distantly they detected the reddish stain of the herd on the prairie. A couple of miles ahead, Larned and his foreman jogged on toward the cattle. As they proceeded, Rowson observed the herd come into formation for the nooning. He made the spot at Nogales Spring, a lean oasis of trees surrounding muddy water.

Cover was slight. Gullies veined the desert, which was broadly level but rumpled with low, transverse ridges. While he studied it, he discovered a rider stringing a thin pennant of dust from the northwest in the direction of Frontera. A last clue went into place in his mind, like a peg in a cribbage board. Bob Hamma was

119

moving in — with his dislike for shenanigans above the border.

He said tersely: "Let's get moving. That female's crazy enough to go to war with the Mexican army and all the cow-town marshals in Arizona."

He pulled the horse off left, winning the protection of a run of hills. Lyndon pulled in at his side. "What's Hamma got to do with this?"

"Hamma's just a lever. Larned's the weight. Larned's buying that herd, not some Mexican wet-beef dealer. Those cattle will be back in the States by tonight, heading east or west . . . away from this range, anyway."

Lyndon chewed on it. "I heard Manteca had big connections."

"Maybe he used to have. Noriega says even the rebels don't trust him any more. So Larned needed a man, and he looked like the one. He could talk big and strong-arm his way into a herd. Then he disappears, and he doesn't come back to Frontera with the rest of those ignorant ranchers' money. Manteca sells to Larned for a few dollars a head, more than he'd get out of a *peso* deal, and Larned brings them back. He's got bills of sale on them and the brands are all right. Everything's all right, except that a few thick-headed *gringos* lost their shirts."

"And he ain't got a bill of sale on Abbie Gaines," Bat finished.

They rode for twenty minutes, and Rowson rode up a hill to get a line again. The herd was sprawled near the spring, only a half mile west. He estimated the cattle at close to a thousand head, most of them Abbie's. Three cowpunchers of Manteca's drifted slowly about the herd as it grazed near the meager spring branch. Flood seasons had cut the water course ten feet deep, a raw slot in the earth, and a little burro grass grew in the bottom of it.

The horseman coming from Frontera was pulling closer to the huddle of men in the shade of the trees. Rowson turned back. "Let's get into that barranca," he said, "and move in as far as we can before they see us. There's apt to be smoke when they do."

They came around the hip of a ridge and sloped toward the gully. Cattle grazed along the banks of it and some were clumsily sliding into the gully for the better graze. A few hundred yards off, the cowpunchers, three steeple-sombreroed men with serapes over their shoulders, drifted along the fringe of the herd, turning the stragglers in toward the water. Rowson put his pony down the crumbling bank, stiff-legged; it struck the sand, and he turned it upstream through a tepid inch of brackish water. In succession, Noriega, Bat, and Angel lunged into the barranca and followed him.

Reaching the cattle, they moved quietly through them. Cattle would stand for a horseman, where a man dismounted would booger them. Page heard the *vaqueros* talking a short distance from the bank. He raised his rope to flog a steer out of his way, but he held his arm and in a tight-lipped patience wormed by it.

A horseman thudded into hearing; there was an exchange of voices. Rowson spurred the pony against an old bull and shoved past. Hamma sounded displeased, but his words were lost. Then the girl's voice came peremptorily, carrying with feminine candor.

"Why should I pay you any money? What for?"

Rowson shoved and hauled through the reddish roil of cattle choking the gully. The barranca was shallower now, tapering into the pond called Nogales Spring. Again he lost the marshal's words, but Abbie cried: "I certainly won't pay a dollar! Who do you think you are . . . the collector of customs? Besides, we aren't even in the United States any more!"

And now Manuel Manteca's voice could be heard: "No, señorita. We are not in the Es-states . . ."

Rowson could see them. There were Hamma and Jay McQuilty, the girl's foreman, Manteca, Shackleford, and Larned. McQuilty, rough and dark, was suffused with angry color. "None of your Mexican hoorawing for us, Manteca!" he said suddenly. "This is a business deal. You go to throwing any of your weight around and I'll hammer a slug through your belt buckle."

"No, señor." Manteca laughed. "This is, indeed, Mexico, and in Mexico the gringo's voice is soft."

"Soft, eh? Soft?" Abbie cried. "See here. I suppose this is a hold-up of some kind. I have to pay Hamma before we can go on with the cattle. Well, you're in this as much as I am, because you won't get any of that money back if the cattle aren't delivered. So it's to your own interest to handle him as I say."

Rowson saw them all begin to look at Larned. The lines had run out and they waited for him to improvise.

Larned — his eyes apologetic under the thorny brows, his manner that of a guilty hound dog — smiled at the girl. "I'm sorry about it, ma'am. But these are rough times. A girl don't savvy cattle, and she don't need a stake like a man does. I'm buying these cows, you see. I'm taking them east to El Paso."

Still she did not comprehend. "Oh?" she said.

Vance Larned rubbed the lever of his .44 caliber Henry against the saddle horn. "From Manteca. He's the real owner of them now, you know. We've got to pay Hamma a little, and it's only right. He could make trouble with the customs people." Larned grinned at the marshal. "So relax, Bob. We weren't running a sandy on you. Only we wanted to make some time, this first day."

"You were makin' it," Hamma growled.

Larned squinted down the gun barrel at a cow, not meeting Abbie's shocked stare. "We didn't want to cut you off clean. So Manuel paid you a middlin' price. I'd take that money, if I was you, and head straight for Guaymas. Get a boat for Frisco. Forget it all."

Rowson saw the terror in her face. He heard the reedy break in her voice. "Forget! I . . . I'll go straight back to the Snaketrack and tell Page Rowson, and he'll . . ."

"No, ma'am," Bob Shackleford said.

The pressure on Jay McQuilty was great. He looked undecided whether to sacrifice himself to appearances, or to wait. He appeared to prefer to wait, for he did not reach for his gun.

Manteca slapped his paunch affectionately. "It will be the great pleasure of Manuel Manteca to escort the *señorita* to the port. I have many connections, *Dona* Abbie. We pass pleasant times, eh?"

Abbie put her hands over her ears and screamed. The men looked nonplussed. Manteca's face distorted. He raised his hand and struck her in the face with the backs of his knuckles.

"*¡Bastante!*" he roared. "We make the good deal, and you es-scream like a she-wolf."

Then McQuilty's somnolent, miserable eyes found Rowson shucking out of his saddle and coming up the bank with the trap-door Springfield in his hands. McQuilty's eyes all but shouted. Suddenly he rammed his pony into the rump of the Mexican's big grulla. Manteca swore at him and made a threatening gesture toward his Colt. Rowson paused on the rim of the barranca. There was a strip of trampled earth fifty feet wide between him and the outlaws, the smoke trees at their backs.

He jammed the butt of the rifle against his shoulder, notched the Mexican's shirt front in the sights, and triggered. The shot trembled hugely in the air, a cannon blast of .50-caliber fire. Manteca was slugged sidewise out of the saddle. He went overboard, and the horse began to kick at his head as he hung by one foot from the stirrup.

Larned saw it all in a stark, comprehensive glance, the quartet surging up over the bank of the gully, guns prodding before them. He sprawled out of the saddle and lay in the dirt. He lined out his fifteen-shot Henry,

124

and Rowson wished bitterly that it were in his own hands. He had emptied his single-shot Civil War gun and now, sprawling in the dirt, he pulled his Colt. He heard the smashing impact of the cattle buyer's shot against his eardrums. It had almost a physical force, a smoky thrust against the eyes. The bullet slammed off the ground beside him and slapped his boot. He felt the sting of it passing down his calf. Screaming, Abbie Gaines rode down the creek.

Shackleford spurred for the trees. But in a moment he halted and turned, afraid to stay and afraid to go. His vacuous, swarthy face was twisted queerly. Angel, lunging behind a shallow rise of ground, threw down on him with his ancient, muzzle-loading musketoon. The .69-caliber ball howled out of the barrel in a cloud of black powder that riffled the ground before it. Shackleford took the shot in his hip; it caught him like a fist and whirled him. He went out of the saddle, moaning, hunching grotesquely with his face against the ground.

Earing back the hammer of his Colt, Rowson was aware of Marshal Hamma sitting twisted in his saddle with his hands up, tallow-white. "All right, boys!" he kept saying. "All right!"

Larned swore and fired the Henry at Noriega, but the *hacendado* lay flat as an empty sack on the ground. The bullet passed over him and *thocked* into a steer. Larned quickly levered another shell into the chamber of the carbine. A gaunt-jointed figure, he sprawled in the dirt with no apparent worries about the odds against him. Rowson rested the heel of his hand against

125

the earth and pulled a bead. But the blooming roar of another rifle shook him and for another moment a smut of black powder smoke and dust obscured Larned. Rowson fired into it and cocked again, but as the dust cleared he saw that Vance Larned had rolled over on his back. One knee was drawn up. He was making convulsive movements with his arms; a man was glad to turn his attention quickly to the marshal.

Hamma was saying: "This is Mexico, Rowson! You can't take me back for . . . for something that happened . . ."

"No," Rowson agreed. "We wouldn't even have you back. We'll tell them about you, though, and I hope you like it down here." Then he got up. "How many of you on your feet?" It turned out all of them were. Rowson said: "Then, one of you bring me a hatful of water."

Abbie came back presently. Rowson's undershirt had been bound about his injured leg. The bullet had created a seven-inch trough in the calf. He was trying to get his boot on with no success.

Abbie said: "It will have to be split." She took his pocket knife and cut the boot down the back so that he could pull it on. Rowson caught Bat's eye.

Bat told the others: "Best git those cows headed back."

Now it was quiet among the trees, and Abbie knelt beside him. "Oh, Page! I should have listened to you."

"You bet you should."

"But I was so sure . . ."

"Were you?" Rowson asked.

Abbie looked down. "No. I knew he might be a cow thief. But you were so overbearing about saying I couldn't do it . . ."

"That you had to show me you were your own man," Page finished. He moved so that his back was against a tree and pulled her to him. "If you had a man of your own," he said, "you wouldn't have to act like one, would you?"

Abbie was sobbing softly, but her fingers roved the short hairs on his neck, causing chills up his back. "No. I guess not," she said.

"All right," Rowson said. "You've got one."

OUTCASTS OF REBEL CREEK

Frank Bonham seldom wrote traditional cow-country stories. On the few occasions when he did make cattlemen his protagonists, he placed them in unusual settings and developed the tales in an unconventional fashion. The locale in "Outcasts of Rebel Creek" from *Dime Western* (12/47) is the high-desert country of eastern California, in the shadow of the vast escarpments and glacial ridges of the High Sierras. Hole-in-the-wall outlaws who have taken refuge in the area, the roughest and least-traveled in the state, are but one peril facing Red Sargent, his cattle baron uncle, Big Red, and other local ranchers. A crafty state senator, a hardcase town marshal, and a greedy cattleman who operates a mountain store that caters to the long-loopers provide additional menace. Fast and furious action is the keynote here, culminating in a pitched gun battle in the fluted parapets of Summit Glacier, with "Death smiling in benediction over the whole scene."

CHAPTER
ONE

His whiskers were like wire and the razor made him wince as he sat there in his camp by a desert creek shaving with cold lather. He stopped suddenly and stood up as he heard horses running. Six riders swung from the stage road into the wagon track leading to his camp. They came at a high lope with their dust engulfing them.

Red Sargent smiled. His hair and whiskers were black, but his mother had named him for her favorite brother, whose hair was roughly the color of a cinnamon bear. Red was twenty-one and hardly a boy now, six feet one and heavy in the shoulders and chest. Uncle Red must have been watching all the trails into town, Red thought, since he had made camp only twenty minutes ago.

The Rebel Creek gang pulled up in a fog of dust on rearing horses. Uncle Red threw off first, coming at Red with a cowman's stiff-legged walk and pulling off a buckskin gauntlet.

"You young varmint!" he roared. "You said the Eighteenth. This is the Twentieth."

He hung onto Red's hand while he looked him over with tears in his eyes. He had the sentimentality of the

Irish, and besides that he had brought Red up as his own son. He was a gentle ruffian who babied his wife and browbeat his cowpunchers. He had big ears, a short nose, and a square chin.

"Got held up by a sandstorm," Red told him.

"What do you think we been havin' here . . . sea fogs? Get them whiskers off and we'll be about our business."

Which would be taking the town apart plank by plank. Cross Anchor men did not often descend from the mountains; when they did, they made the hours count.

Red ran his palm over a smooth cheek and liked the slick, civilized feel of it.

Uncle Red, watching him, said: "Gettin' stout. Another year up with me and you'll be flankin' your own oxes."

"Not sure I'll be here a year, Uncle Red."

"The hell with that!" Sargent snorted. "Your aunt's got your old room ready."

Red didn't answer. They started for Torreón. It was good to ride with the old bunch again. They were taciturn men, but they showed their friendliness in ways Red knew.

Short of town, the Mojave stage went by with a grind of iron tires. Someone leaned out of the window to wave. There was a vague familiarity about the girl's face.

"Who was that?" Red asked.

"Shore makin' connections," Uncle Red said, and grinned at the others. "That was Shelly Challender."

"When'd she start riding the stages?"

"Her daddy's doin' pretty good," Big Red Sargent said off-handedly.

It was coming close to the thing Red had to know before he made any plans about staying. "How are things up the hill?" he asked.

Uncle Red removed his Stetson and replaced it over one eye. They were coming into town. "Why, pretty fair, Red. Pretty fair."

"Whose beef you eating now?"

"Challender's. Senator Wheeler got too rich for my blood. All shorthorn."

"Things pretty quiet?"

Uncle Red cleared his throat. "Been pretty quiet," he said. "But they aren't going to be for long?"

"Hard to say. Wheeler came back last week with an appropriation to spend during his vacation. He's going to civilize the High Sierras. He says."

"What do you say?"

"He tried to once before, you recollect. That was on his own. This is with a state grant, but I don't figure fellers are going to be much happier to die for a buck just because it's been blessed."

He spoke thoughtfully. He was a deep-voiced, slow, and guilty man, Red had seen it grow on him, this diffidence about meeting your glance, and he knew it was because of Rebel Creek.

When it began to grow on Red, this guilt disease, he had left the ranch and hired out on a cow spread near Los Angeles. He was a son of the mountains, and it had not been easy to go. The Sierras stood up like giants

133

from the earth, ribbed with rock, almost devoid of timber. Most of their peaks and ranges were above timberline. There were ghosts in their passes who screamed and crooned and laughed.

They made men queer, although in different ways. Uncle Red had the glory of them in his eyes. Senator Tom Wheeler felt little in their presence, and he had got into the habit of shouting when he thought they could hear him; so naturally he wound up in the state senate. And Ord Challender had learned their craftiness and could ride across rock slides few men could, and he could shoot a rifle straighter than anyone Red had ever known.

Since it was the roughest and least-traveled area in California it was popular with outlaws. They could take a bunch of stolen cattle in and pasture the critters in a mountain meadow, or they could merely hole up under the groaning ledge of a glacier until they were ready to leave. This required the co-operation of the ranchers who owned the area. If they left a sack of grub near a roost and forgot having traded horses with somebody who rode by in a hurry, they were pretty sure to find some money in the ashes of an old campfire. It was a fairly steady source of income with some of them.

Wheeler had made an ass of himself, during a burst of religion, by setting out to clean up 100,000 acres of crags. His men deserted after a night attack. Wheeler lost his horse and came back half-starved and raving. He had never appeased his humiliation. Red was not inclined to sympathize with him. He had come to know a great many outlaws, and, as men, he liked them. Most of them talked about not having received a square deal. Maybe they hadn't, but in a business like this you had to play the cards you held, and the cards an outlaw dealt were smudged with blood. Your blood, if you were caught harboring them.

Lately the mountain country had been getting a name in California for what it was — a hole-in-the-wall. It was close to the gold fields, to the borax towns, to the cow towns and farms. Someday the law was going to come in a pack, and it would go hard with ranchers who had too many off-brand horses in their corrals. That was why Red had left. He had come back because he was homesick, and because he was lonesome for a girl. He had promised himself never to think of her after he left Rebel Creek. But, as a matter of fact, she was about all he had thought of . . .

The Mojave stage had dropped two passengers and their baggage. The station agent was handing up the way pouch as the Cross Anchor crew came in at their fanciest trots. A blonde girl stood on the walk, watching them. She wore a blue gown set off by lace at the throat and wrists, a gown that nipped in at the waist so that a man could have spanned it with his two hands.

Shelly Challender had changed a lot as to exterior, but she was as bold as ever. "Red! Come over here," she called.

Red winked at his uncle. "Meet you boys *poco tiempo*."

Uncle Red's hand curled the brim of his hat. "You bet. Oh, Red! You knew her and Stan Horn are engaged?"

"No, I didn't . . . Thanks," he said.

Shelly took both his hands. "Red, why didn't you tell us you were coming back?"

"I didn't know it myself until a couple of weeks ago. Thought I'd make sure the hills were still here."

"The only landmark we've missed was you," Shelly said. "Going to carry my bag to the hotel? Dad's supposed to be down to take me home tomorrow."

It was a hot day in late spring. They walked along under the giant elms. Shelly had an arch sort of walk he didn't recall, something compounded of her own wild grace and the knowledge that even men who were too shy to watch her coming turned to see her pass. She had become quite a show-piece. He guessed she was becoming civilized.

"How was L.A.?"

"All right. Too big."

She looked up at him in the personal way she had. Red was a little sorry that she had got herself engaged to a stuffed badge like Marshal Stan Horn. Even if his times with her had been to spite another girl, she had been fun.

Suddenly Shelly's hand moved on his sleeve. "Why, there's Stan!"

Stan Horn came down the steps of the jail, a big, dark-browed, simple man with a head like a buffalo, a belly cut by a beaded belt, and guns that pronged from his hips like the horns of a polled Durham. He wore a pony-skin vest and a flat-crowned Stetson set back on his huge head. Torreón had kept him in office because he maintained the peace in saloons courageously, and that was about all there was to it in this sunburned town under the blue eaves of the Sierras. He raised Shelly off the walk while she scolded him, kissed her, and set her down. He regarded her the way some men looked at a steak.

"By golly!" he said, examining her dress. "You bought 'em out, didn't you?"

Shelly began to straighten her dress. "You haven't said hello to Red."

Horn stared a moment. "Well, I'll be danged! Where did you come from, feller?"

"L.A. How many times have you had Uncle Red locked up since I left?"

Horn began to figure. "Let's see. He took on a load after the rodeo last fall. Then he come in the day after Christmas . . ."

"I'll take your word for it," Red said.

Horn gave him a blinking study. He turned to Shelly. "Your daddy's going over to Bishop tomorrow. Like me to ride up with you?"

Shelly was getting that cat sound in her voice. "You're sweet, Stan. But Red's going up, anyway. He's offered to take me."

Red stared at Shelly, ready to shake her until she bawled like the freckle-nosed urchin she was. But he was unable to say anything, while the marshal rubbed the back of his neck and thought about it. Suddenly it dawned on Horn that he was being stood up.

"But you said last week . . ."

"I didn't know Red would be coming in, did I? And tomorrow night's Saturday, and you ought to be around."

137

Red said stiffly: "I may not be going up tomorrow, after all. Better figure on Stan."

"I'll bet I can talk you into it." Shelly laughed.

They walked on.

"That was nice," Red growled.

Shelly giggled. "I've got to keep him guessing, haven't I? Besides, if I let him take me up there alone, I wouldn't be safe."

They reached the hotel, a shaded, two-story adobe structure on a corner. A decaying flunky took Shelly's bag inside. She held Red's hand an instant, her eyes laughing at him. She had displeased him, and enjoyed savoring it.

"By the way," she said, "Gail Wheeler and the senator are staying here, too. I know she'd be glad to see you. She sees so much of the Sacramento crowd that she'd probably get a laugh out of watching a cowboy make love again! They say she used to . . ."

CHAPTER
TWO

Red watched her go in with a pert swing of her hips. The hell with her, he decided. She could escort herself to the ranch.

Horn was still on the walk in front of the jail. He stared as Red passed, threw his cigarette into the street, and went inside. Red rejected the notion of explaining. The marshal was a man without flexibility, a born grudge-holder. He affected a hearty manner and bragged of his strength, but his eyes were ashamed of too many things.

In the vacant lot beside Howey's General Store, two men sat on the tailgate of a wagon. A cigarette made a red arc in the early dusk as one of the men waved.

"What's the hurry, Red?"

Ord Challender dropped to the ground and came forward with his long, articulated gait. Shelly had taken on gloss, but her father looked more lean and unprosperous than ever. He resembled a trapper at the end of a hard season, a bitter-eyed man who, if he could not change a thing, knew how to put it to his own use. He had made an asset out of the ragged range where he ran cattle.

Will Mullan, his ramrod, joined them and they shook hands. After a moment Challender said to Mullan: "Run up and tell Shelly we're staying over a few days, will you? Red and I'll be at the Dragoon."

Ord put a casual hand on Red's shoulder as they walked. "So you found your way back. Any plans?"

Red was uncomfortably conscious of the hand on his shoulder. "Just looking things over," he said.

"So are some other fellows." Challender chuckled. "The senator tells it mighty scary."

"I get the idea you've been doing all right, Ord."

Challender watched their boots tread the walk. "Pretty nice," he said. "Hear about my trading post at Grand Pass? I carry a little likker, shells, and corruption like dried fruit and hard candy, sort of things a man gets to hankering for when he's been on the trail too long."

"Shouldn't think you'd get much trade up there, off the beaten track."

Challender shrugged. "Transients, you know." Then he laughed, and clapped Red on the shoulder. "Red, I missed you," he said. "You got a sense of humor, something that damned fool Shelly's picked out ain't . . . I had a notion you were sweet on her once."

"I know when I'm well off," Red said. "Life with a tornado might be too rough for me."

"In fact, I thought I might get you as a son-in-law someday," Challender persisted.

Red stopped to light a cigarette, but mostly to get rid of the cattleman's hand. "You wouldn't like me as a son-in-law. I'm too religious. Even Uncle Red's too wicked for me."

"Now you're jokin' again," Challender said. "Seen the fighting marshal of Torreón? We're going to put the greased pig under him at the election next week. He's been all right up to now, but things are different."

"Is that any way to treat a son-in-law?"

They were near the crowded hitch rack of the Dragoon Bar. Challender stopped in the shadows to face Red, his sour, gullied features tense. "Listen, boy. I'm not just testing my wind. I can swing plenty of votes in this county, if I set myself to. I'll get people out that ain't voted since hell froze over. I like Stan, but even his mother'd have to admit he's slower'n Adam's off ox. We like the hills just about like they are, Red. We mind our own business, and that's no skin off anybody's nose. But when a U.S. marshal takes a look at Stan, he figures, if we really wanted the mountains cleaned out, we wouldn't have a feller like that in office. And on top of that, a change would look good. Red, I know more about you than you do yourself. You can follow a trail over pure granite, and I figure you could lose a trail in wet sand, if you thought the man ahead of you hadn't been given a square deal."

"Wait a minute," Red said. "You aren't going to suggest that *I* run for marshal!"

Challender grinned. "Ain't I?"

"My God!"

"No fooling," the cowman said, "you could walk into the job without working up a sweat! You'd be good for

141

us. And, well, there's no reason why we couldn't do you some good, too."

"You're talking pretty plain, Ord," Red said.

Challender held him by the elbow. His sharp features had an unwonted vitality. "That's it! I can talk plain to you because you got savvy! You could hold that job three years and then quit and buy yourself a ranch or something. If I gave out the word that you were riding through, they'd hang gold pieces from trees along the trail. You know some of them boys anyway, Red, and . . ."

Red made a motion with his arm that shook Challender's hand loose. "I'm sorry you opened up, Ord," he told him. "I used to think I could take you or leave you alone. Now I've got to be pretty careful to leave you alone. When they start hanging cowmen in the Sierras, I don't want to be rattling spurs with you from a high limb."

Challender's reaction was not plain. It fell short of anger, but not far short of disdain. He reached up to rub his chin with a knuckle. "Anyway," he said carefully, "I've given you something to talk about, ain't I?"

"Don't worry about that," Red said. "I won't be bragging about one cull mistaking me for his brother very soon."

There was a party in the Dragoon that evening, with Uncle Red setting them up. Around nine o'clock, Challender called for a deck of cards and a bottle, and took a table.

Red decided to get something straight with his uncle. "Keep this under your hat," he said. "Challender made me a proposition this afternoon. He says he can make me a rich man in five years . . . as county marshal."

Sargent's face congested as though he had swallowed a fishbone. His thick fingers strained around the whiskey glass as he turned from the bar toward Challender's table. He put the glass down and took one step into the room, but Red hauled him back.

"I said it was on the quiet," he snapped.

"The dirty, sin-festered, low-livin' . . ."

"That's what I wanted to hear." Red grinned. "Now I know you've stopped harboring long-loopers. I suppose you've got a quiet hour, too, when you read the Bible and pray?"

"Cut it out, Red," Sargent said gruffly. He turned back to the bar, savagely swirling the liquor in his glass until it spilled, then throwing the rest down his throat. "That stinking son!"

Red was sorry he had opened up, but he wanted to look at the picture entire, and he asked softly: "When are you going to take in the welcome mat, Uncle Red?"

The giant of Rebel Creek grunted. "Once you've put it out, you don't take it in. They'd cut off my ears. They'd kill all my cattle."

"Somebody's going to cut off your ears if you don't."

Sargent cocked an eye at Red in the backbar mirror. "If Wheeler goes in there again, he'll come out roped sideways across a pack mule."

Someone passed them, heading none too steadily for the door. Will Mullan, Challender's foreman, shoved through the door out into the warm spring darkness.

"Then you'd better get out while you can, hadn't you?" Red asked Sargent.

"Yeah? How do you get off a running hoss without getting skinned?"

"Slow it down first."

"I'd like to. But other fellers keep whipping the hoss up. You know about Challender's trading post? That's just one angle. They're thick as thieves on my range as well as his. Red, I'm worried. I'm glad you're back."

"I'm not back until you give the word that we put the screws on them."

Uncle Red shook his head slowly. There was a commotion at the front. They saw Will Mullan come inside again. He stood there, a crudely made Swede who appeared to have been constructed of two-by-fours, his eyes accusing the saloon.

"Some gazabo," he announced, "has stole my hoss!"

There was a stir in the room. The bartender drifted up and men began to leave their places at tables and the bar. Sargent's voice went calmly through the racket. "You're crazy, Will. I moved it around to the side of the building a while ago."

Mullan stared. He came along the bar and stopped to lean on it by one elbow. "You moved my horse? Why?"

"Because yours is a stud, and mine's a stud, and any damn' fool ought to know better than to stick them side by side this time o' year!"

144

Mullan rubbed the flat of his hand over a beer ring. "That's a matter of opinion. I've been tying studs next to horses and mares for thirty years, and I've had no trouble yet."

"I have." Sargent, appreciating the low comedy of the situation, began to grin. "You're a big man, Willy boy, but you aren't so big as all this . . ."

Uncle Red stood six three, weighed 250 pounds, and yet had a waist no thicker than Red's. While Mullan was still scowling, his right hand grabbed a fistful of the ramrod's pants, his left took his collar, and he barreled the Swede down the floor and out into the street. There was a splash from the water trough, and Sargent came back, laughing.

"Crazy son-of-a-bitch!"

He had not quite reached Red when Mullan returned, drenched and wild. He snatched a bottle from a table and came at a shambling run toward the cowman.

The bottle made a fair target. Red, standing behind his uncle, fired twice, the second shot shattering the brown glass. Will Mullan looked at the jagged stub he held. Even this did not sober him. He shifted it as though the club had become a knife. He came on.

Red let the barrel of his Colt tilt down, but Uncle Red snapped: "I can handle him!"

His hand swept a schooner from the bar into Mullan's face. Mullan dropped, covering his face with his hands. Blood began to ooze darkly from a cut across his eyebrow. He lurched up again and rousted a man out of his way to face the cowman across six feet of sawdust.

"Let's git the Cross Anchor sons!" he yelled.

An Anvil man answered with a mustanger's yell. Others picked it up. Red saw them beginning to stir in the crowd, looking for his uncle's cowpunchers. Something less than a feud, but more than a grudge existed between the outfits. It gave a little sauce to their days in town to look forward to a fight, and it furnished range conversation when they got back.

Red watched Mullan tangle with his uncle. He saw his head rock and Mullan fell against the bar. Open-handed, Sargent began to slap him about the head until the ramrod's face was fiery and he staggered.

Across all this violence of shouting and fighting, Red looked and saw Ord Challender at his table, nodding pleasantly to himself as though he were watching a bronc'-stomping contest which pleased him. He saw Red standing apart from it and gave him a look that said he approved of that, too. Red felt awkward, standing there. Why he wasn't fighting, he didn't know. Maybe because he instinctively realized he wasn't part of the old crowd any longer.

Mullan lay in the tawny, rumpled sawdust, while Uncle Red sucked a cut knuckle. The other fights were going briskly. It was an effective time for Marshal Horn to arrive.

He stood just inside the door with his hands on his hips. "All right, boys!" he shouted. "All right, damn it, break it up!"

The racket thinned. A couple of men who had not heard him continued to roll on the floor. Two men dragged them apart, and they both looked a little relieved that it was over. Stan Horn came through the tables with a hint of swagger. He knelt beside Mullan, then he glanced up at Uncle Red.

"Who started it?"

"He said his pop could lick my pop," Uncle Red told him.

Horn grunted and threw a glass of water in the ramrod's face. He hadn't looked at Red yet. He stood up. He tapped a table twice with his forefinger. "Too early in the evening for this. What's going to happen when you larrupers get likkered up? I'm taking your guns in, you Cross Anchor and Anvil men. Pick 'em up when you leave town."

Uncle Red laid his gun down. Challender crossed the saloon to place his beside Sargent's; it was a .44 with the bluing rubbed off the highlights. Horn amassed thirteen guns. For the first time he looked at Red. "I'll have yours, too."

"Deal me out," Red said.

"What do you mean, deal you out?" Horn was wearing his shotgun voice. A relish was turning over in his eyes. "How do you figger . . . you God or somebody? You're Cross Anchor, and I'm taking yours with the rest."

Red said: "I haven't taken a job, yet, and it may not be with Cross Anchor when I do."

Ord Challender's eyes glinted with sardonic humor. "That's right, Stan. He just stood there."

147

Looking at Horn, Red was sorry he had started it. The marshal had backed himself into a corner now. He hadn't the nature to admit a fault, and his slow, sensitive mind was confused with all the wrong emotions, pride and embarrassment and anger for what Shelly had done to him.

"I want that gun," he said suddenly. He grabbed a gun from the table and started for Red with dark-red fury in his face.

Uncle Red made a quick grab and had the gun out of Horn's hand. He laid it on the bar. "Not that way, Stan. If you're trying to settle something, that don't show here. Why don't you do it like a man? Both of you leave your guns and go outside. We'll wait here."

Horn realized a middle road had been opened to him. He pulled off his badge, lifted his gun from the holster, and laid both on the bar. He walked past Red toward the back entrance. "You come along," he said.

CHAPTER
THREE

The vacant lot behind the Dragoon was tufted with small desert shrubs and formed a cemetery for several hundred dead soldiers form the saloon. Horn was waiting for him, a hunch-shouldered from in the warm night. He was silent while Red approached, and then profanity began to pour from his lips.

Red cut into it. "We're being a couple of jokers, Stan. I'm sorry about Shelly, but there wasn't anything I could do. It was her party."

"Get it into your fat head that this ain't about Shelly!" Horn snarled. "It's about a damned, big-mouthed cowpoke that thinks he can run this town better than I can!"

"I figure I couldn't run it any worse," Red remarked.

One thing he had never given Horn credit for was craft. That was his mistake. Horn's hand jerked and dirt stuck Red's eyes like buckshot. He was momentarily blinded by the sharp grit under his lids. He pressed his hand over them, swearing at the pain and at Horn.

From nowhere a rock seemed to explode against the bridge of his nose. He went back, with Horn atop him, slugging his head and bringing up a high-driving knee. The sickness of that blow to the belly doubled Red up

149

on the ground. He heard Horn coming in and hunched against the kick, but the marshal must have denied himself that pleasure. He began to curse him, daring him to get up.

Red's tears washed a little of the grit out of his eyes. He could see Horn hunched over him, his fists tight against his sides. He took advantage of the marshal's reluctance to kick, and let him swear while the cold weakness ran out of him.

Horn sucked in an eager breath as Red rose. He went in again like a bulldogger tackling a steer. He jolted Red with a right to the brisket, tagged him on the ear with a left, and had another right cocked when he suddenly gasped and tried to avert his face. From four feet away, Red flung an overhand blow. It missed by two feet, but the rocks and dirt he had come up with exploded in the middle of the marshal's face and left him stumbling backward through the brush.

Red laughed, softly and wickedly. "Hell of a trick, ain't it, Stan?"

Horn turned and faced him blindly. He grunted as Red's first punch smashed his lips and nose. He raised both hands to keep him out of range. Red side-stepped and slugged him on the ear. When Horn staggered away, he caught him by his shirt and tore his face with three hand-axing blows. Horn swayed and reached, and Red brushed his arms aside and let his shoulders follow up the punches he threw into Horn's body and face. They smacked sweetly and there was the feel of no lost motion, just the swing of his shoulders and the bruising of his fists.

150

Then Horn was no longer before him, but lying huddled on the ground, stirring slowly as he tried to rise. Red helped him up with a hand under his belt. Then he helped him down again by jolting his head with an uppercut that tipped Horn's face to the sky.

Starlight gleamed on his cut, bleeding face. It shook Red to see what he had done, but there was the taste of blood on his own mouth and he knew he would not be pretty in the morning, either.

He left Horn lying there half-conscious, and, walking uncertainly because he was not quite right himself, went to the hitch rail and got his horse and rode out of town.

That night he slept beside the creek, heeding the good sense it talked. The sun on his face turned him out. His right eye was closed and his upper lip was puffed. He felt like the dirtiest, lowest pit in hell.

Three cups of coffee failed to straighten a mind that was cluttered like a postmaster's desk. He wished he'd let Horn have his victory, to suck on like a lemon drop. He needed it. Red didn't.

He wished he had not met Shelly; he despised her and yet recognized in himself a little of the champagne tingle she put in a man's blood. He despised himself, then, for not having better taste in women. But, actually, he did. He thought of Shelly's remark about Gail and was sore again.

He rolled his blankets and tossed a pack saddle on the mule, and now there was a moment when he thought: *The hell with it! I'll go on.*

He was seeing himself as Shelly had wanted him to, as a lumbering cowpoke tracking dirt into Senator Wheeler's parlor and sitting at the end of the sofa while conversation died the death of a dog. A proposal from such a character ought to be worth a guffaw in almost any salon in Sacramento where she recounted it.

His own common sense straightened him out on this. She was too kind to laugh at a man either to his face or behind his back. She was kind and gracious and vital, and he'd be damned if he didn't have the same kid infatuation with her he'd had two years ago. In the soil of a dozen letters, it had grown like a weed.

He peered at his lumpy visage in the steel mirror. A pretty sad face to take courting. Still, he had three months to work, until the legislature reconvened. By that time, he'd know where he stood . . .

He rode into Torreón. Uncle Red had slept in a back room of the saloon. By custom, nights before were treated like dead friends, often thought of, but seldom mentioned. Sargent said merely: "Coming up with us this morning?"

"Later. Will you be at the place?"

"Not for a few days. Got some calves to wean on the way up."

It was not yet eight o'clock. Red waited outside the restaurant until it opened, and almost the first thing he saw was Gail coming in from the hotel side. She took a table and he watched her eyes rise to him as he approached. She saw his bruises and laughed and shook her head.

"A fine way to let us know you were back! Why did you do that to Stan?"

Red took a chair. "Why did he do this to me? Where's the senator?" he asked her.

"At the lodge." Gail's eyes — cool, gray, and knowing — were laughing. "She *is* pretty. But no girl is pretty enough to fight over."

"Almost any girl is," Red corrected her.

"You've never fought over me."

"I'll take care of that this summer," Red said. "Where can I find that Sacramento fellow?"

Now it was her turn to color. A waiter came and she hurried to order.

As they ate, he made the discovery that she had become easier to talk to. To him, she had always been two people. Up on Despair Meadow, where her old home was, she was a dark-haired, vivid-lipped girl who wore short skirts and loose blouses. She was a quick-moving creature without fear of horses or men, who knew when to look out for them. But in town, she was a graceful young woman in decorous dresses who carried a parasol against the fierce summer suns of the Mojave. She was a pretty but slightly mysterious girl. She managed her father's houses on Despair Meadow and in the state capital with efficiency.

"Will you do something for me, Red?" she asked suddenly. "Dad was coming down for me on Saturday, but I'm ready to go up now. I've got all this stuff to take up, and I thought, if you could pack the mules, I could handle them myself on the trail."

"I'm going up, anyway," Red told her. "The lodge will be right on the way."

Her luggage was behind the hotel. Red got mules from the stable. When Gail came out, she wore a brown, leather riding skirt and one of the blouses he remembered, white, thin for coolness, with a deep neckline. She had tied her hair back with a red ribbon. In two years, she had hardly changed — a little more sober, maybe — her figure a little fuller.

They ascended through tumbled foothills into Cottonwood Cañon. At the head of it, they started the abrupt ascent. The Sierras stood vast and austere about them. The trail forded a stream and slanted upward along a thousand-foot rock slide. Wheeler's ranch was the most westerly of the Torreón group. It was rugged range, but ended against Uncle Red's, where the real mountains began.

Big Red Sargent ran his cattle in a hundred-thousand-acre wilderness following the southern slope of the Inconsolable Range. Ord Challender's was the great, whispering hinterland of rocks and tiny lost meadows and furtive streams beyond the Inconsolables. From a ridge they surveyed the senator's main pasture, an irregularly shaped carpet flung among mountains and the wreckage of mountains.

Red was heady; he didn't know whether it was emotion or the altitude. Gail asked: "Like this country, Red?"

He shrugged. "Always have, up to now."

"Afraid somebody's going to spoil it?"

154

"Maybe somebody already has."

Gail looked at him. "You talk like a man Dad could use."

"Big Red Sargent's nephew? The senator used to claim I was brought up on his beef."

"Maybe that's why you understand things your uncle doesn't. You could help, Red. You know these mountains better than anybody but Ord Challender."

Red did not reply, and they rode down into the basin.

As they were unsaddling, the senator rode in. He dismounted, an erect, gray-bearded man with a strong nose and a firm, lined face.

"Been too long, my boy!" he boomed in his big politician's voice. "You're looking fine, though. You'll stay with us tonight?"

"Well, I hadn't . . ."

"Nonsense! Won't have it any other way."

Wheeler took charge of him. Red couldn't figure it out. He was plied with good Scotch, and then there was a fine meal on the verandah of the stone ranch house overlooking Despair Meadow. The plates cleared away, Wheeler rolled a cigar between his hands. "I suppose," he said, "you've talked to your uncle."

"I've tried to. I think I know what you're going to talk about, and I can't help."

"How do you know you can't?"

"I don't know any more about what goes on in the mountains than you do, and I'm not going to guess. I talked to Uncle Red about running Cross Anchor like a good hotel . . . nobody to get in without baggage and registering. He says it wouldn't be practical."

"Why wouldn't it?" Wheeler snapped the question and his mouth had a harsh set.

Red shrugged. "It's no business of mine how he runs his ranch."

"You'll just sit in the middle of the forest fire and pretend it isn't getting warm, eh?"

Red smoked and made no answer. The senator got up and stood at the railing with his hands clasped behind him. He cleared his throat several times, and finally turned back with the cigar vised in his teeth.

"Would you feel any different," he asked, "if you had . . . ah . . . legal authority to help me out?"

It had a similarity to another speech he had listened to recently. Red smiled. "Are you going to elect me marshal, too?"

"Too?" Wheeler looked surprised.

"Somebody else thought I'd make a good marshal. I'm pretty sure he votes the other ticket, though. Is that what you had in mind?"

Wheeler, off balance, went on with less drive. "Well . . . yes. I figured you might feel this way. And I need a man like you, Red, who knows those cañons and understands the men we'll be dealing with. So I planned to invest you with the power to go after them. How about it?"

"I wish I could. But if it comes to trouble with Uncle Red, that's where my allegiance belongs."

Wheeler stood erect, staring down with his old dislike. "Then that's all I need to know, isn't it? Good night."

156

CHAPTER
FOUR

At 10,000 feet, the nights were frosty all year around. The cold, thin air carried the slightest sound like the click of a firing pin on a shell. It was a series of sounds that awoke Red. First he thought it was a horse, then he decided it was a couple of colts cavorting in the corral, and then he heard a high, frightened trumpeting. Footfalls began to sound through the house. He saw Wheeler, wearing pants over his nightshirt and carrying a lantern, go out into the yard. A moment later he heard his startled shout.

"Lon! Gail!"

Lon Kittredge, his foreman, was plunging out of the bunkhouse, tucking his shirt tail in, when Red ran down the steps. Near the corral, where the lantern made an island of yellow light on the earth, a scuffle was in progress.

Red got the picture as he ran up. A pinto horse was resisting the senator's efforts to remove his saddle. Red got the pony's ears in his hands and dragged its head down, and now he saw that a man's foot was still in the stirrup, and beneath the horse hung the form of a man, limp as a rope.

Kittredge and Tom Wheeler freed him while Red held the pony by the cheek strap. Red led it around, and turned it into the corral. He heard the senator say: "Go inside, Gail."

In the freezing night, Red stood near this man who lay crumpled on the ground. Rocks and hoofs had all but torn his head off. His face was obscured by blood and dirt and dried scraps of weed.

The senator, on his knees, was panting: "God! God!"

Kittredge, a wiry, gray-haired little man, was hanging onto a corral bar. Red closed his eyes. Before him gaped the picture of a dead gopher, choked with dried blood and weeds and showing two upper front teeth.

Wheeler stood up. Standing there, his arms hanging straight down, he said: "This is the first, but it will not be the last."

"Who was it?" Red asked him.

"Joel Kane. I sent him into the Inconsolables last week."

"Alone?" Red asked.

"I thought . . . never mind what I thought," he said. "Red, do you still think Big Red Sargent is running nothing but cattle over there?"

"I don't know what he's running, but I know anyone should have had better sense than to send a rep alone into that country. We don't even send a cowpuncher out there by himself. If he had a fall, he likely wouldn't come back. That's what happened to Kane. Did you look at his saddle? The horn was cracked. The horse probably fell and Kane was knocked cold, and there was nobody to stop the pony from running."

Kittredge, gray and shaken, gave him a glare that was a copy of the senator's. "You don't reckon it could have been a bullet that knocked him out of the saddle?"

"If it was," said Red, "we'll never know. The top of his head's gone and there's no blood on his body."

Senator Wheeler shook himself. "What's the matter with those men?" he barked at Kittredge. "Turn them out, every man jack of them! We're taking the trail tonight. I'll do my investigating from the back of a horse!"

"Your eyesight's better than mine," Red said, "if you can quarter a talus slope in the dark."

Wheeler looked at his watch. "It's three o'clock. We'll have daylight in an hour and a half."

He strode back to the house.

Returning with his carbine, he saddled his gray and mounted while five stunned cowpunchers also saddled. He passed down the line like a cavalry colonel on review. He confronted Red, who had mounted, too.

"I'm warning you, Red, this is a hang-rope posse! If I find any indication that your uncle's in this, I'll take him in, dead or alive! If you want to go along, understanding that . . ."

He swung his horse so violently it reared and came back to cut from the yard in a digging lope. The others hurried to follow him. Red paused to acquire the lantern.

A faint star shine brimmed in the valley. The line of riders drifted through the turns of the meadow trail toward the eastern rampart, a phantom cavalcade with no greater tangibility than the rasping hoofs and the frequent explosion of iron on rock.

They halted while Wheeler dismounted to study sign. Red had extinguished the lantern. Finding what he wanted, the senator swung back into the saddle and they rode in through a grove of red fir. He continued along at a fast, clopping trot. The trees ended and they were high above the valley on a steep pitch that merged into giant rubble from the palisade above. The trail was a tenuous thread among boulders.

There was a fork here that only the accustomed eye might discern. Wheeler knelt and failed to read the trail. From a box of matches he extracted two and struck them simultaneously. The flame gasped out in the wind. He lost three more matches. He sat on his knees in perplexity

Red called to him: "Like a lantern, Senator?"

Down the line of heaving ponies Wheeler stalked to yank the lantern from Red's hand. In the lee of a boulder, he lighted it. Now he was able to see that the horse had come from the upper trail to Gault's Ridge.

Nearly an hour later they topped the ridge. A gray light was seeping through the cañons. Wheeler turned victoriously to announce: "This trail leads just one place . . . Sargent's main pasture!"

They followed a narrow cañon where a stream fell noisily over the rocks. Now they caught the odor of wood smoke, and Wheeler slowed his horse. And in that moment a rifle tore the air apart and the lantern vanished with a splintering of glass. Wheeler was piling off his horse with a breathless yell. The cañon rang with the echoes of a hidden battery. There was gun flame and the reflection of gun flame on the wet boulders of the stream. There was the roaring of ponies and the swearing of the men trying to control them.

Red saw all this, and he saw that no one had been hurt. So it was no surprise to him when Big Red Sargent's voice called from the boulders.

"Reckon you boys took the wrong turn somewhere. You just head back the way you came and you'll be on your own ground again. And a whole lot safer."

Cross Anchor men began to come from behind the rocks. In the strengthening daylight, they bunched at the bend of the trail and watched Sargent walk to meet the senator.

Wheeler began to shout: "You damned fool, you might have killed someone . . ."

"I still might. You didn't used to come freighting a gun when you called on me, Senator."

"I've never had one of my men murdered on your range before."

"Murdered!" Sargent said quickly. "You don't mean Kane?"

"You seem to know what I'm talking about."

The irritation of too many hours with Wheeler began to gall Red. "Senator," he said, "you've messed things up about enough for one night." He told his uncle: "Kane's horse dragged him in at three o'clock this morning. His head had been pretty well battered up by the rocks. His saddle horn was cracked, and it looked

161

like he'd been thrown and dragged. So we start out to hang somebody."

"Under ordinary circumstances," Wheeler retorted, "I might have been deemed over-suspicious. But I'd sent . . ." He hesitated, and Uncle Red laughed softly.

"That's all right," he said. "I've had him tracked since the day he came. One of the men brought him to the weaning camp for a remount last night. His horse had gone lame. I let him have his choice of the bronc's and he picked a pinto that was boogery about squirrels. But he was like you, Senator . . . you couldn't tell him nothing."

Wheeler grunted in surprise. "But you don't know what happened to him after he left your camp?" he persisted.

"I can make a good guess. The horse shied at something and went down. Kane was dragged."

Without a word, Wheeler turned to his pony. In the saddle, he lingered to stare down at the cowman with one hand on his hip. Red got the impression that he spoke too much from platforms.

"There's nothing I can do but take your word for it, Sargent. But one of these days I'm coming up with a search warrant and a young army, and you'd better have your long-looping friends off this ranch by then, because there won't be a cave or a thicket we'll miss! That's a promise."

Sargent threw back his answer as the senator rode away. It was a ringing crash of laughter that made Wheeler's ears burn.

★ ★ ★

The weaning over, Sargent that afternoon sent the cows down-cañon and drove the weaners to a higher pasture as they rode on to Cross Anchor headquarters.

As they topped out into the wild upland of lush meadows and lean ridges, Red told him: "That was Fort Sumter you took this morning. Don't forget it."

Sargent's flat, hard face with its sandy stubble darkened. "Let the big-mouthed fool bring his fancy lawmen. I'll give them a show."

"And probably hang for it. He's outfitting for an army. I saw crates of shells and a ton of canned grub over there. He's got a map on the wall with pins in every possible hide-out. He's done a pretty good job of spotting them, too."

Uncle Red started to say something, but his lips clamped on it. He chewed the idea for a long time. When they reached the divide above the valley of Rebel Creek, he told Red to take the calves on. "I'm going to shake hands with some old friends."

Red stared at him.

Uncle Red smiled. "That's right. I was a pretty tough *hombre* with Wheeler, wasn't I? Let's see how I make out with somebody that's got all his faculties."

"I didn't say you should ride out alone and put the screws on them!" Red exclaimed.

"I can't go any other way without asking for trouble."

He rode up the trail that followed the ridge to the base of the Inconsolables. Red left the herd with a cowpuncher and followed him. Sargent did not speak.

"Who's in camp now?" Red asked him.

163

"How should I know? I hear Charlie Hannigan left a chunk of his ear with a Wells Fargo messenger last month, though. Got a twenty-thousand-dollar borax payroll." Uncle Red chuckled. "Charlie sure used to like the trout in Black Lake, didn't he?"

For an hour they rode through scattered stands of pine and fir, to drop down a dry cañon that debouched into Black Lake. Around sunset they entered a tule meadow at the south end of a small reach of water bordered on the west by cliffs. Above the cliffs were sandy, open spaces among the trees, and back a little farther a section of basaltic caves.

There was a tang of wood smoke in the cool air; they caught a luscious odor of frying trout. A thin pencil of blue-gray smoke rose from the jack pines near the caves, and now there were three quick shots that hammered out, and the soft plunking sound of bullets falling into the marsh was very near.

As they rode toward the trees, Uncle Red began to whistle "The Campbells Are Coming".

They reached a campfire. Upon three blackened stones balanced a sheet-metal plate that supported a skillet full of brook trout and a bubbling coffee pot. Saddles lay about and three tin plates had been left on the ground. Uncle Red speared a fish with his hunting knife and stripped the pink flesh from the backbone with his teeth, and, while he stood there, three men came back to the fire.

One was a big, round-shouldered man with a scabbed ear and a face like a rock. He grinned at the cowman. "Howdy, Red. Whyn't you say you was coming?"

"Thought I'd surprise you. How you boys making out?"

"Swell," Charlie Hannigan said. He grinned at Red. "Howdy."

Red nodded. He placed one of the other pair, an ugly, near-sighted little outlaw with a small face under the brim of a big hat. His name was Otto Tripp; his past was a trail littered with old dodgers and Wells Fargo rewards. The third man was a stranger, a solemn, brown-mustached man with the look of a country parson.

"Hope you haven't exceeded the legal limit on fish," Sargent said sardonically.

Otto Tripp cackled, Hannigan roared in his haw-hawing bass, and even the mustached man smiled.

Uncle Red lifted his hat and scratched in his Airedale-like wiry hair. "Just thought I'd see how you were fixed up. Don't need anything at all, then?"

Hannigan's gaze was a steady one with a crease of curiosity. "Not a thing. Ord takes care of our vices."

"All but one, anyhow," Tripp corrected him.

"I was going to say," Sargent remarked, "that, if there is anything you need, you can buy it in Carson City. That's out of my jurisdiction, and the state's, too. Healthier for all of us."

Tripp was the one who stiffened, understanding fully, but Hannigan said mildly: "We like it pretty well here. Thought we might stay till fall."

165

"I wish I could let you," Sargent said. "But Tom Wheeler's back with a state appropriation to clean us up. They'll hang anybody they catch, and any rancher convicted of harboring will go to San Quentin."

Hannigan laughed and stirred the fire. "I've been hearing that yarn for years. I'm ashamed of you, Red, letting them buffalo you this way."

Big Red said doggedly: "They mean business! I'm saying you . . . you better think about a new spot, Charlie."

Hannigan shook his head. "Nice of you to tip us off. But we'll take our chances, hey, boys?"

Tripp poured himself a cup of coffee. "We can't do anything *but* stay."

"Preacher?" Hannigan said. Somebody besides Red had noticed the resemblance.

Preacher shook his head. "Leaving the mountains would be knotting our own hang ropes."

Hannigan looked back, spreading his hands, and Red spoke for the first time angrily: "We're not asking you, Hannigan . . . we're telling you. You've had a soft thing for years, but it's over now."

"It's been soft for a lot of people," Hannigan said, looking at Sargent.

Uncle Red began to heat up. "You've got full value for anything you ever gave me. That is, if you figure your neck is worth anything."

"Worth too much to move along right now," Hannigan grunted. "I'll promise you this . . . if they come, I won't be around."

166

"You won't be around next week," Red snapped. "We can't take the chance. They may come any day."

Hannigan gave him a jeering glance. He spoke to Sargent. "The kid thinks he's pretty tough, Red."

"Maybe he is. I think my twelve men are tough enough for the three of you, if it comes to that. And I don't aim to finish my days weaving gunny sacks in a penitentiary. We've been *amigos*, Charlie, and I hope we still can be. But we've got to break it up."

Tripp stood up from the fire, and the Preacher, sitting cross-legged, contemplated them while his hand rested on his thigh just an inch from his Colt. But all Hannigan did was lean forward and lift a crisp-fried trout from the pan by the tail and twist the head off.

"OK. You're the boss, Red. Going to miss the old place, though."

Sargent, mounting, softened. "Honest to God, I'll miss you boys, too! You're a bunch of lugs, but damn' pleasant lugs. So long, Charlie. So long, fellers."

They rode out casually, but with nerves strung like a new barbed-wire fence. They reached the cañon and turned into it. From the outlaw camp there was no sound at all.

Uncle Red blew out his cheeks. "By George, maybe you're right! For a minute, though, I thought we were dead ducks."

"There's a lot of wind in any of them," Red said sagely.

"A little less in Hannigan than most."

It was nine o'clock when they came into the ranch yard. They ate wearily and turned in.

Sometime in the black, silent hours a horse whickered. Shortly after, a window shattered. There was a crash of breaking china, and then the woods beyond the ranch yard were illuminated with rippling stabs of orange-yellow flame.

CHAPTER
FIVE

Red was sleeping in a room at a corner of the ranch house. Two walls were covered with shelved preserves. Trunks were stored here, and Red's Aunt May had fixed his bed under the window. He rolled onto the floor and crawled to his carbine. A shot passed through the window, smashed a jar, and filled the room with the sharp incense of homemade pickle.

The bunkhouse was at the rear of the main structure. The cowpunchers were in action already, pumping their fire into the trees and rocks. Red lay on the cot and rested the barrel of his Savage on the sill. He waited for a flash. When it came, he got off a snap shot. He could barely discern his front sight. It made aiming a matter of instinct.

He heard his uncle roaring encouragement to the men in the bunkhouse. He estimated a dozen rifles in the woods. Hannigan had not come alone. He had sent out the word, and the pack had responded.

What Red Sargent wanted to do right then was to square things with his uncle for having turned the wolves loose. He had talked everlastingly big, but without thinking it through. And now he knew that because you take pot luck at a man's campfire, you have not necessarily savored his philosophy. He had assumed there would be a leavening of gratitude for past favors to mellow the outlaws' resentment. Big Red's protection had been merely a matter of value received and nothing more.

Another slug slammed into Aunt May's preserves. Red slid off the bed and left the room. He stood in the kitchen, hearing from the parlor the massive booming of Uncle Red's .45-70 and his aunt's calm advice. "Now, Red, keep your head down! They'll leave as soon as they think they've throwed the fear into you."

From the window, he scanned the brush beyond the rear yard. He saw no gun flashes, and noted that the windows on this side were intact. Red opened the back door and stood inside it a moment. Then he darted through. Running lightly, he reached the buck brush, where a hill broke the flatness of the meadow. He found the old split rock where as a boy he had hidden so many times during imaginary Indian fights. The cleft in the rock was a tighter squeeze than he recalled, but he got himself wedged down with a collection of smaller stones for a parapet.

The flashes of the guns were close, from here. Back in the trees, he thought he discerned a light-colored horse moving. He turned the .30-30 into the trees, emptied the magazine, and saw the firing line fall dark. Somebody was swearing.

Red reloaded swiftly. Before he was through, a bullet slapped the rock above him, startling him so that he spilled half of his handful of shells. He crouched lower and tried to concentrate on punching cartridges into

170

the magazine, but he was shaking inside. Copper-jacketed hell was hammering at the slot.

Then the ranch yard was silent, except for the *wham* of Uncle Red's heavy caliber rifle. Red suspected that his own gun was an unexpected factor in Hannigan's raid. Again he laid his cheek against the cool walnut. When the gun began to buck, there was definite reaction from the trees. Two guns spat back at him, but the rest were silent, while the brush snapped under hurried boots.

He heard the deep bark of his uncle's gun once more; before the hills finished tossing the echo a man cried out. When a man was mortally hit, you could tell it. There was a stricken quality in his voice. The cry Red heard had that sound.

The last two gunmen ceased firing. A long wait passed with only whispers of movement and the groans of the wounded man. Finally Red heard horses moving distantly. He waited ten minutes longer and ducked back to the cabin.

They spent the night near the windows. The wounded man stopped crying out just before sunup.

By daylight they found him, a nameless man lying huddled across his gun with a handful of spent shells about him. They buried him on the spot. They went back to breakfast, but no one ate much and no one talked.

Finally Uncle Red made an announcement. He did not look at Red.

"I used to do my own thinking. I recollect that I got along pretty well. I aim to try it again, and here's two ideas of mine you can pin up where they'll be handy. We don't ride less than three to the bunch from now on. If you run across anything that ain't a cow or a horse, and you don't know it, shoot it. We're going down to vote next week, and I hope the man they hang the marshal's star on ain't a friend of mine. I'm short of friends already. I've had my little fling at crusadin', boys. I'm plain Big Red Sargent again, and that don't leave no explaining to do."

With four men, he disappeared into the crags.

There was a pressure on Red to leave, an understanding that the old, exhilarating days were dead. But he remained, more willing to outstay his welcome than to be accused of deserting.

Sargent returned on the morning of the election. He looked at Red with amazement, and then his eyes filled with a sultry fire and he told him he wanted to see him alone.

He walked to the feed shed. In the misty gloom of its interior, they faced each other. Sargent's breath came through his teeth.

"I thought you savvied after last week that I wouldn't be cryin' when you left. I'm saying I'm sick of your psalm-singin' preachments, and this is how I'm saying it!"

His fist cracked against Red's cheek bone, knocking him back against the wall. Red staggered away and automatically put his hands up, but his uncle was finished. He turned, and his wide shoulders crowded through the door. Red saw him leave with half the Cross Anchor crew a few minutes later.

172

It didn't take Red long to roll his blankets and ride out. He was angry and defeated. He felt he had bungled, and yet he had done what he had to. Riding along in this mood, he heard someone call him and looked up to see Gail on her pony at the side of the trail.

"Red, what in heaven? You said you were going to stay."

"They yanked the welcome mat out from under me," Red told her.

Gail swung down off her pony. Red followed her over to the stream. "Now, what's happened?" she demanded. "You and Uncle Red didn't used to fight."

"I didn't used to preach the gospel according to Sargent. It . . . well, it didn't work out." He smiled at her concern. "The mountains aren't moving away. Just one 'puncher. And next fall you'll go back to Sacramento and let them drink champagne out of your slipper and forget all about it."

The sunlight was quick and glinting in her hair as she shook her head. "I had to quit that," she said soberly. "I got tired of going home with wet feet."

Red laughed, but Gail's smile was lost quickly.

"Red," she said, "will you do one more favor for me? Run some cattle back to our range?"

"What cattle?"

"Some registered white-face calves. Dad found a tally book in Kane's pocket in which he'd listed all the strays he found while he was on your uncle's range. It was an odd thing that they were all blooded heifers. I know Uncle Red didn't move them and I don't think

Dad really believes it. But some people would say he was going to get some calves out of them before he sent them home."

"That's Uncle Red's worry."

Her gray eyes, light and intent, didn't let his go. "It's my worry, too. Dad's gone down to talk up Lon Kittredge for marshal. If he wins, he'll come in with deputies to find those cattle. If Horn wins, Dad will come anyway, with his own reps. Either way there's going to be trouble, unless the cattle are sent back. They're in Shorty's Cañon. Will you drive them out . . . for me? It means a lot to me, Red!"

"Putting it that way," Red said, "sure. I'm always a set-up for a girl that wants a favor done. When I was thirteen, a girl wanted a hair bridle. I liked to skinned my uncle's black cutting horse and the old white plug my aunt rode out for the milk cows. But I made the bridle. And what do you think? She never used it."

For a moment Red thought she was going to cry; there was that pre-tears look to her face. She didn't, but her smile was as wistful as tears. "And she never will use it. It's too beautiful. She hung it on the wall of her room. It must have taken a month to make."

"Three months," Red said.

"I take it to Sacramento every fall. It's a little piece of the mountains that I can put in my suitcase."

"You're going to miss them after you get your assemblyman, or judge, or whatever he is," Red said.

Gail took hold of the top button of his shirt. "Let's get straight on something. My assemblyman is

174

forty-eight and he's an important man. But when he eats, his face gets red and he slicks his hair down across his bald spot like a doily. He's Dad's choice, so, of course, he hasn't got a chance."

Red was relieved. There was a sort of singing in him. He held her shoulders lightly in his hands. "I'm a very small eater myself," he said. "And my hair's thick and your old man hates me. Don't ask me why I don't make out better than I do."

"Maybe you aren't ambitious enough." Gail laughed. It was a soft laugh you couldn't have heard ten feet away.

Red's hands tightened and she closed her eyes as though she knew what was going to happen. He suddenly held her roughly in his arms and kissed her; he felt the warmth and the softness of her lips against his.

Quite a while later they walked back to the horses. "Still going away?" Gail asked him.

"Got to. I can't fight Uncle Red, and, if I stay, that's what I'm liable to be doing. I'll give the boys six months and come back again."

"You'll stop at the lodge when you bring the cattle over?"

"You bet," Red said. "Will your old man be there?" He suddenly grinned at her.

"He'll be gone until tomorrow. But there's Juana, the cook."

"Give her a glass of blackberry brandy and we won't have any trouble with her," Red said.

175

Gail laughed. It was the most intimate laugh he had ever heard. He wondered what there was about it that made him tingle.

CHAPTER
SIX

Shorty's Cañon was five miles from the ranch. Red left his pack horse in the corral and started out. His guess was that Hannigan, or one of the others, had left the calves there to be picked up later. From a side hill he saw a smudge of smoke near the ridge of the Inconsolables, at Grand Pass. It occurred to him that from there, with the glasses, he might be able to pick up some things worth knowing. And then, too, he was curious to see Ord Challender's trading post before he left.

The steep drag to the 12,000-foot summit had the horse laboring. The impact of a thousand winters had stripped from the mountains everything but stone and wind and tatters of old snow. Above the gap, on the west, soared the broken battlements of Summit Glacier, its vast talus tapering out in a graveyard of tumbled markers behind the round rock hut in the pass.

A rag of smoke whipped from a rusty stovepipe in the roof. Red saw someone step from the doorway with a rifle in his hands, and he halted the horse and returned his careful stare. Then he saw that it was Shelly, wearing denim pants and a short, doeskin hunting coat. She leaned the gun against the hut.

He came on. Shelly watched him put a rock over the reins. "I don't know whether I'll let you stay or not," she pouted. Red laughed, and she said, still resentfully: "I had to get a hostler to pack me in. You wouldn't, and Stan couldn't."

"Whose fault was that?" Red asked her.

He began to walk toward the hut. Shelly shook her head. "I'm so sick of sitting in there I'm about to start talking to the chipmunks. Let's sit up here and see who can count the most outlaws through your glasses."

They sat on a boulder above the hut. All the vast wilderness of Ord Challender's range was at their backs, while Red put the glasses on Black Lake, to the east.

"Where's Ord?" he asked.

"Where's everybody? In town for the election. Why aren't you down? I thought you were going to be our next marshal."

Red lowered the glasses. There was something intense in her manner, a sort of glitter about her. "I'd have to give up my seat in Congress," he said. "I decided to hang around today and see if I could find out who shot the hell out of Aunt May's preserves last week. How's the trade in shells been?"

"Good. I thought I heard the racket. It sounded like the opening of the deer season."

Red watched a chipmunk trying to summon courage to enter the hut. It sat on its haunches and scolded. "It was the opening of hunting season on lonesome cowpunchers," he told Shelly.

"Anybody hurt?" she asked casually.

178

"Nobody that mattered."

Shelly looked down into the basin of Rebel Creek. "There may be some people hurt who do matter, before it's over. If you were smart, you'd get out. You don't have any stake here."

"Sure about that?"

Shelly sniffed. "You don't think she'll have a blue-jowled roughneck like you, do you?"

Down below, the chipmunk advanced to the door of the trading post, and again retreated, chattering. "She might," Red told her. "Devotion. That's what counts with a girl, Shelly. And I'm devotion right down to my spurs."

He stood up, letting the glasses hang against his chest.

Shelly said archly: "Are you?"

"With the right people," Red said. "That's why you'd like to kick me off this cliff, kid. Because I treated you the way you deserved the other day."

When he started down the hill, she stood up quickly, to remain there with her fists clenched. "Where are you going?"

"Down to the hut!" Red called back. "I'm curious to know why that chipmunk is afraid to raid your grain bin. I thought I smelled one of Stan's cigars a minute ago, too, and I'm wondering if he's in there, or if you've taken up smoking stogies."

Her features were small and pinched. "I wouldn't, Red. I'd get on my horse and ride . . . fast!"

Red walked to the hut, stopping a few feet short of the door and trying to see into the gloomy interior.

179

Inside the shack, someone moved. Red saw Horn lumber into the doorway, then he was aware that there was another man with him.

Suddenly he staggered and slapped his hand to the back of his head, where it seemed a monstrous bee sting had penetrated his skull. He slipped to his knees and the world about him was as bright and pearly as the interior of a soap bubble. It shimmered and smiled, and suddenly it burst, and beyond the opalescence there was darkness.

He could hear them talking about him. He thought: *You muffed that one, buckaroo!* It had only been a few minutes since he left. The light was the same; there was warm blood flowing down into the collar of his shirt, and the position in which he lay across the doorway was one from which they would have moved him before long.

"Damn it to hell!" Horn said. He sat on a rock, staring at Red.

Charlie Hannigan's bass rumbled cheerfully. "You're just one of them fellers born to worry. Time you rode down, anyhow. Be 'most night before you can make it. He won't be here when you come back."

Red sensed that the marshal was in the position of all small men who play for larger stakes than they can afford. He was faced with plunging, and quailed from the idea.

"Do we have to . . . do that?" he asked.

Shelly said in a vixen voice: "No! You can let him ride into town and say you and I are living together up here,

180

and Charlie Hannigan boards with us. I'll bring you hard candy on visitor's day."

Hannigan was philosophical. "Well, I don't know. I figure he had it coming. He started the whole thing, you might say."

Red was becoming increasingly aware of things, and one of them was Shelly's carbine, leaning against the wall not far away.

"I guess so." Horn sighed. "I guess you're right. It . . . it did look like he was going to pull a gun on us, didn't it?"

Hannigan chuckled. "You got the right idea, Stan. Only I wouldn't say 'us' when I told it . . . I'd say 'me'."

Shelly made a disgusted sound. "I'll get your horse, Marshal."

Hannigan turned to watch her pert shape start down the trail. Thus it was Stan Horn who saw the cowboy rear up and make for Shelly's gun in a swift crawl. His obtuse features were slow to catch up with his emotions. They were alarmed, but becoming angry as he got his .30-30 into position an instant before Red hit the ground, clutching the light .25 sporting gun.

"Drop it!" he commanded. But without waiting for effect, he fired.

The bullet went into a fissure of the rock wall. Horn was not by nature a man of action. Red rolled onto his side and directed the carbine with one hand. His first impulse was to take the marshal prisoner, but he saw his hand swiftly operating the lever and knew that action would end in squeezing the trigger. Something in him that hated violence began to tremble as he looked at the spot on Horn's shirt where the bullet was going to enter. The small-caliber gun bucked with surprising energy.

Horn went back, the way Red had heard a man did when hit by a high-velocity shell. He went back and fell across a rock. The hole in his shirt was hardly visible, but blood was welling from the other end of the wound in his back.

He saw Charlie Hannigan begin to draw his Colt. Killing this man would have been less offensive, but Hannigan was a clear thinker who knew when he was finished. He raised his hands shoulder high.

"All right, cowboy," he said.

It was seven-thirty when the little pack train of three horses, two men, and a corpse reached Torreón. Heat still lay in the basin, but there was more than a hot summer's day activity in the town. Voting had ended at seven, and now men were strolling the walks or populating the saloons while they waited for the results.

Someone saw Red's party and let out a shout. They came from both ends of the street to surround the horses. A man exclaimed: "Stan Horn! And Red's got the dirty son-of-a-bitch that killed him!"

Hands were put violently on Charlie Hannigan, dragging him from the saddle. Red stood up in the stirrups. "Take it easy, boys. That's Charlie Hannigan, wanted from hell to breakfast. But I'm the one that killed Horn."

They stared at him without comprehension. Red saw to locking Hannigan up with keys he had taken from

Horn's pocket. When he had finished, Senator Wheeler was in the office. He was in shirt sleeves, with lavender suspenders striping his pleat-front shirt. Doc MacMurtry, into whose life came little of such excitement as an assassinated marshal, greedily saw to the transporting of Horn's rigidly warped body to his office.

"Going to be a hell of a job!" he said eagerly. "I'll send over the truck from his pockets, Senator."

Wheeler had come in from the election committee and was rumpled and upset. He evicted everyone from the office and closed the door.

"Red, do you want to make a statement to me about this? I'm a lawyer, you know. If you think you'll need legal help . . ."

"You can take my affidavit, if you want."

Wheeler took down what Red told him, nodding forcibly as the story came out. He had Red sign it and banged the desk and stood up. "It was all you could do! He knew he was finished as marshal if you reported his friendship with an outlaw, so . . ."

Red was exhausted, mentally and physically. "That's right. I'm going on to Nevada tomorrow. If I'm needed, I'll come back."

Wheeler got a mysterious smile on his face. "You aren't going anywhere at all. Your duty is here." From a slip of paper, he read: "Total votes cast, eight hundred and fifty-nine. For office of marshal, Inyo County . . . Samuel Phelps, ninety-four. Stanley Horn, two hundred forty-seven. Red W. Sargent, five hundred eighteen."

Red stared. "Do you mean to say that after . . . ?"

"I'm not a stupid man, Red, just quick-tempered. I came to understand that you had nothing to do with Kane's death, even if your uncle . . . well, we won't speculate. The point is, I promoted a write-in campaign for you. When you say the word, we'll go to work."

Red wagged his head, amused but disturbed. "I'm not even eligible!"

Wheeler gestured. "Let's not talk about tosh like residence."

"Let's not talk about it at all," Red suggested. "I made the mistake of trying to go back to something. I nearly had my head shot off being convinced that it can't be done, but I'm not going back to let them finish the job."

The senator lifted his chin.

Red cut him off by opening the door. "I'm sorry, Senator. You can pin your badge to the seat of your pants or make a cookie cutter out of it . . . but I'm not having any."

He was in the café a while later when he saw Uncle Red leave town. Challender was hanging around, sour-eyed and vindictive, letting his boys parade about with the arrogance of carpetbaggers in a Dixie town. The word was out that Red Sargent had turned Torreón down.

Cow towns had an inability to hide their feelings about a man. What Red felt was hostility. They had him tagged. *One of the Sargents, all right. And yellow to boot.*

He walked to the hotel. His gear was all at the ranch. He'd pick it up tomorrow and make the loop to

184

Bridgeport. It would be a pleasant ride; he would have such cheerful companions: defeat and loneliness. He remembered when he'd come into this hotel, cocky and optimistic, a walking blueprint of things he was going to do. Purify the heart of Big Red Sargent. Convince a girl she needed a forty-a-month cowpoke for a husband, when she was turning down $5,000 a year in Sacramento. But he knew that in giving up the job, he was giving her up, too.

He got his key and lay in a hot room with the tattered green shades drawn, his arm across his eyes. *Marshal Red Sargent. The hanging marshal. He hangs his head like all the Sargents.*

Out of all this guilt was bound to come self-defense. If he'd had a break, just one break, he'd have led them into those tiny pockets only a man born in the hills would know; he'd have scoured the hills as clean as a new skillet. He thought: *You're thinking too much, Marshal. You need a drink.* He was amazed to discover how thirsty he was. He piled off the bed and pulled on his boots. He hummed a brave tune, "Oh, whiskey, you demon . . ." What could you buy that gave you as much?

The big, rasping Seth Thomas in the lobby indicated eleven-thirty. He strolled down to the Dragoon. A gang of Challender's men were bulling along the boardwalk toward him, rough men in batwing chaps, liking the chime of their spurs and the sound of their voices. They came on at Red like the point of a herd, and then someone recognized him.

They joshed around, but the wedge opened up and no one jostled him as they went past. Stan Horn lay in the back of the doctor's office, tied to a plank, and Charlie Hannigan was staring thoughtfully between bars. Such things made a man think.

Red drank with the quiet determination of a man trying out a new medicine. At midnight he felt a pleasant stirring in his blood. At twelve-thirty gloom began to gather about him again; he recollected a saying of his uncle's that Irishmen should never drink except to start the tears.

At one o'clock, when he had given up, Lon Kittredge, Wheeler's ramrod, came bellowing into the saloon.

"Hannigan's loose!"

CHAPTER
SEVEN

Red went up with the rest to look at the jail. The sill and bars of the outlaw's cell had been yanked from the mud wall by a horse. Whose horse was the question? Men began to recall that Ord Challender's crowd had melted away some time before the jailer noticed Hannigan's absence.

Wheeler stormed down from the hotel. In ten minutes he was whipping a posse together. "They've taken him back into those hills, men. But there's nothing to keep us from going after them!"

Nothing but mountain savvy, Red thought.

Wheeler assembled a posse of fifteen men. The horses caught the mood of the crowd before the jail. Now and then a cowboy would wheel his horse and let it take a little run down the road to untrack it. Wheeler made sure everyone had shells. He rode around in a hell of a hurry.

"Davies, you going to be able to handle that horse?" he shouted.

"OK, Senator!"

"Everyone ready, then?"

Red couldn't sit still and see it happen. He came out of the shadows. "Excuse me, Senator."

Wheeler searched for him. "Oh, Sargent!" he said. "Are you taking the Cottonwood Cañon trail?"

"Is there another?"

"No. But they could cut you to pieces at any of those turns. I'd wait for daylight, if I were you."

"You would, eh?"

Someone called: "Think it's too dangerous, Marshal? Think we ought to stay home with you?"

Red kept his attention on the senator. "How much food are you taking? You may be on the trail a week."

"I . . . I figured to pick up food at the lodge."

"What if the trail doesn't take you there? And another thing. I was wondering how good your boys are with Colts . . . at four hundred yards? You may not get any closer than that, and I see only a couple of them have carbines."

"You know so damn' much . . . ," a rider began.

Wheeler sounded tired. "All right, Red, we're as ignorant as you say we are. Not many of us know the upper trails. But we've got the guts to try them. It takes as much courage to do what we're doing as it would for you to pin that badge on. All we can hope to win is self-respect. But that's all we want."

He had him tagged, Red thought. Probably the old fox had been making as big a botch of things as he could, just to draw him out. He had him by the short hairs. And the surprising thing was that Red had the feeling it had had to end this way all the time. He said good-naturedly: "All right. I'll settle for that, too . . ."

When they finally left, the posse had the look of a military expedition. Red had cut out three of the horses as being too nervous for mountain work. Half the mounts had required shoeing; a loose shoe that would get by in the desert would not last an hour on a rocky trail. Each man carried some food behind his saddle.

Daylight was hot on their backs when they mounted through Cottonwood Cañon. There was sign to indicate a dozen horses. Red made them string out to prevent an ambuscade. He projected himself into Challender's mind. Escape for Hannigan was the label this bore, but it amounted to more than that. It was Ord Challender's declaration of independence. He could get Hannigan out of the hills if he wanted to, but there would be all the smaller men on his range to draw wrath down on his head. Challender had protected them all these years, and now they were going to pay for it.

They had taken the main trail as far as the cut-off to the Anvil. Here the cavalcade had cut up to a ridge above Uncle Red's land. Red knew with certainty now where they would meet them. They were streaking for Challender's home range, for a spot where there was food and ammunition for a small army, and that meant the trading post at Grand Pass.

About a mile from Rebel Creek, he suddenly swung his pony. "Hold it! Somebody in the trees!"

A horse moved onto the trail. It was Gail in the saddle. She came toward them at a lope when she was sure of them. The senator almost rode her down. "By heaven, Gail, do you know who you almost ran into by sashaying around out here?"

"Of course. I heard them go by last night. I rode up to warn Uncle Red, but he was already on the job. He's got his men on the trail a little way ahead, and he swears none of you will go through!"

Red and Wheeler went ahead alone. There was a warning shot somewhere, and they jogged into a long, twisting avenue through the pines, where Cross Anchor cowboys stood among the trees and rocks. Big Red Sargent came into the middle of the trail. He gave Red a sardonic grin, looking at his badge.

"Good morning, Marshal, sir. Out hunting outlaws so early, Marshal?"

"That's right."

Sargent glanced at Wheeler. "And practically single-handed."

"Red, I want to talk to you," Wheeler declared.

"Shore wish I had time. But I've got some hell to raise with Challender and Hannigan. I had a no-trespassing sign on the trail, and somebody shot it and spat tobacco juice on it. But just for the sake of the argument, let's assume that it still stands."

Wheeler's voice lacked all the old trumpet echoes. "Listen, Red. You and I are in trouble. Do you realize that?"

"Is that new?"

"Not by a damn' sight. And yet we've been acting as though it was . . . Red, do you remember the year we came in here? The year of the Paiute War?"

Something flared in the eyes of the giant of Rebel Creek. "Do I!"

"Twenty-five years ago," Wheeler said. "All we had was a gun, a new wife apiece, and a prayer. And once it got so bad we had to shack together a whole summer.

190

After that we had our trouble with cow thieves. Remember? By God, didn't we give it to *them*, though?"

Sargent scratched the back of his neck, trying not to grin. "And I tied one up in a spoiled cowhide and drug him halfway to Bishop! That was about the last of it, wasn't it?"

Wheeler sighed. "Sometimes I wish we could turn back the clock. Times were tough, but we were young and the world was bright and nothing mattered. Well, you can't slow it down. We're old, homely as buffaloes, worth ten times as much at the bank but only a quarter as much in our hearts. And that's why we ought to stick together, Red."

He had touched something in Sargent that only another old-timer could have. Big Red didn't speak, but he began rubbing the barrel of his rifle frowningly. "What've you got in mind?"

Wheeler winked. "Showing these youngsters how we did it during the Paiute trouble! Of course, that was before we got so damned important that we couldn't see each other for tally books and elections. Think we could do it again, Red . . . run the rats to hell out of here so we can sleep o' nights?"

Sargent chewed his lip, and then began to grin. "We could try, Tom. You know what I figger? I figger they've holed up at Black Lake in them caves."

Red said quickly: "Not unless they've got a lot more chuck than we saw the other day. My guess is Grand Pass."

Sargent jerked a thumb at him. "Listen to that, will you? Telling us how to do it already! Still, it's a point, ain't it?"

When they rode, twenty-two strong, they were heading for Grand Pass.

It was noon when they crossed the last rock slide and saw above them on the west the fluted parapets of Summit Glacier, a thousand feet of splintered granite against a clear blue sky. "Now," Red said, "we take it slow. The tracks show they came this far. We'll know pretty soon if they went any farther."

Three men were appointed as horse holders while the rest went ahead on foot. The trail came out in a field of gigantic rubble at the foot of the talus. Dead ahead was the short pitch through the pass to Challender's trading post. There was no smoke from the rusty iron chimney.

Pacing slowly in the lead, Red was thirty yards ahead of the next man when he heard a cry behind him. He was hitting the ground even before he turned, and, as he did so, he heard the rattle of lead against the rocks and flung himself behind a sharp-edged boulder. Down from the base of the cliff slashed the fire of a staggered line of rifles.

CHAPTER
EIGHT

The wounded man lay there, trying to drag himself behind a rock, but no one could help him. Uncle Red started toward him, but the slugs raining about him forced him to shelter. Afterward there was no point in taking the risk again, because the cowpuncher had taken another slug and lay on his back with a wound in his head.

Now and then a rifle crashed and the sound was first a loud and startling crack, and then a cascade of shattered echoes pouring into the pass. Then there would be the aching stillness of the high altitudes, the sun bright and heatless, and Death smiling in benediction over the whole scene.

There were bursts of firing from both lines, but no one was hit. The men below were having trouble aiming high enough, while most of Challender's crowd was firing high. Then there came a time when the jacketed lead began to fall closer. Once Red looked up to recognize, even at a hundred yards, the ugly head of Otto Tripp above a boulder, round as a melon. He made the best shot he ever had, and was almost sick when he saw the bullet's red, fruit-like creation.

There was the beginning of fire from the hut. Red had not even considered it, but someone inside was firing calmly and steadily along the line of possemen, and having good luck. One man sank down with a splintered forearm and three others had to hunt new rocks. That brought a storm from the heights, and Red watched rigidly as they flopped and hugged the boulders.

He thought, this can go on for a week. He drew a bead on that section of the rock wall where he thought the firing was coming from. He saw a faint smut of smokeless powder just where he was aiming. He squeezed off the shot.

The scream was muffled but high, and it went into Red's heart like a stiletto. Shelly would be in it, of course! She would be fighting like the little savage she was, but God, oh, God! why did he have to be the one to hit her? There was that one cry, and then the hut was silent.

It could go on for a week, he thought again, but it wasn't going to. He could have drawn a topographical map of that post-pile glacier. A mountain climber had come through here once and said that Glacier Summit was just a walk, but the time Red Sargent climbed it, he had thought he would never get down again. And that was without a rifle. He'd be carrying a rifle, this time. The only way up was around the back way. He could make it to the shoulder that jutted out over the basin in three starts.

He broke from cover like an antelope, took a dozen long strides, and piled behind a boulder. They hadn't

194

even fired a shot. His heart was slogging from the exertion. He flapped his Stetson out the right side, and then slapped it on his head and ducked out the left. Their fire sprinkled the pass wildly. He wound up behind the hut and after an instant's breather sprinted on.

Someone up there must have got too eager and exposed himself. Uncle Red's big .45–70 bellowed and one of the outlaws came head-over-hip-pockets down the rocks. But Red Sargent was around the hump.

The climb was a two-hour struggle up natural stairways, across shelving sides, through clefts where he looked down on 500 feet of air before he got to safety. He had fastened his belt to his carbine and carried it along under one arm. He was skinned, winded, and sweating when he realized he was near the summit. Before he could go on, he had to lie there and let his lungs gasp hungrily at the thin air.

From below, the spires had looked sharp as needles. Actually they were broken stone pillars five times the girth of a man. He gazed down the long, dizzy slope to the bottom. They had been waiting for him. He saw the thin blossoming of their powder smoke, and then lead *whanged* off the rock, reassuringly distant.

The disadvantage was that he was too distant to get in any good licks himself. He scowled over this, and that was when he leaned on a balanced rock and scared himself by rocking it. He caught his breath, began to grin, and pushed it again. It rocked like a cradle. Two tons of rock, aching to be gravel on a talus slope! He tried to tip it over and failed. Then, the marksman in him groaning, he got the barrel of his Savage under the rock and heaved. It stirred, half pivoted, and began to roll.

He heard it *thud*. The thunder of it was a magnificent thing. Shouts of startled gunmen were still more gratifying. Red began to roll everything in sight that could be budged. In between rocks he stood and landed a few shots as close to the outlaws as he could. He could make out Ord Challender's drawn-wire frame hunched between two rocks, while Charlie Hannigan knelt on one knee and continued to fire upward.

But the others were getting ready to break. He could see the motionless bodies of two men who had been felled by fragments. Another tilted boulder challenged him. Red sent it hurtling down, saw it shatter in a fine dust of rock powder among the trapped men.

A man jumped and ran toward the cattlemen, firing his Colt. Others caught the fever and started down through the rocks. Even Challender joined them. It was Charlie Hannigan who stood up last. He did not run. He stood there and fired his rifle until they dropped him, and Red knew with a horror that he was shooting his own, deserting men.

In the black, bitter night they returned to Cross Anchor. They carried their wounded and dead, Shelly one of the latter, and drove the captured Anvil men and outlaws ahead of them. There was a fire in Uncle Red's comfortable stone ranch house. When they neared it, they could smell coffee and frying bacon.

196

Red was a little longer than the rest in unsaddling. Before he was through, Gail came out. She found him leaving the corral.

"Let's not go in there yet," she said. "It's noisy, and I want to be quiet. I want to be quiet and listen to you tell me what you're going to do for the next twenty years."

"It may take about twenty years to tell that," he said. "Would that be all right?"

"All right," she said.

DUSTY WHEELS — BLOODY TRAIL

As the previous stories have shown, Frank Bonham used a variety of offbeat, historically accurate settings for his Western stories. El Paso during the Civil War, in which hotels bulged with stranded travelers, and the perilous road south to Mexico City are the scenes in "Dusty Wheels — Bloody Trail," which originally appeared in *Dime Western* (6/49). Entrepreneurial freighter Jess Clyman purchases thirteen stage-coaches, ten wagons, and seventy-five horses and mules from the Great Southern Overland Mail, with the intention of driving them to Mexico City for resale. A young woman whose father is the Confederate American consul-general there, a rough-and-tumble Great Southern section boss, a doctor with a lynx eye, and assorted drivers, teamsters, and meat-getters accompany him on the long journey. Bandits, hostile Indians, Southern sympathizers, and other hardships make for a tense, colorful narrative so vividly recreated the reader can almost hear the creak of thorough braces and harness leather, smell the trail dust and powder smoke, feel the harshness of the landscape.

CHAPTER
ONE

Men who play a waiting game need an accurate sense of timing. Clyman had this. They require boldness, and he had this. Originality is not out of place, nor capital, if they hope to sweat out the other fellow's game, and these things, too, were his. Jess Clyman, twenty-eight, unmarried, quiet but vigorous, knew he'd need all these attributes if he were to bull his way through this grandiose scheme of his, and he had decided, with a young man's vanity, that there was nothing he lacked.

For two weeks he had lain around El Paso, spending most of his time in a fuming little gambling and drinking place called El Sueco. He sat at a front window, with a view of the wind-harried plaza and the stage station across the way, watching the packing-in of a transcontinental log jam of stagecoaches, wagons, travelers, and horses. Hotels bulged with frightened men and women. Saloons thundered with talk of war. Travelers journeying east were dumped here because the stages would go no farther for fear of running into bands of raiding Southerners or Black Republicans. Travelers following the western star were left high and dry because the Apaches had hacked to pieces most of the line between El Paso and Tucson.

201

El Paso was a cage full of terrified human animals who did eccentric things, who killed one another nightly out of sheer terror, with cards or women as an excuse. Jess Clyman felt himself aloof from the mood of panic. He had the indolent polish of self-sufficiency. He had a bag of gold, and, when the time looked ripe, he'd walk across the plaza to the depot of the Great Southern Overland Mail and make his proposition to the division superintendent.

He was a dark-skinned, blond young fellow with blue eyes that looked pale in his dark face. He had been born in Missouri but raised in the Mother Lode of California. Given the figuring, it had not taken him long to notice that the men who had the gold were not the ones who dug and panned for it. They were the men who served them. When he was old enough, which was seventeen, he bought a span of mules and a wagon and began freighting on a small scale. By the time he was twenty-seven, he had run it up to 25,000 dollars' worth of animals and rolling stock. Then he got the urge to travel, and he put his money into gold and started east. He was one of the men who had been jettisoned at the El Paso depot. In three days he knew what he wanted to do.

He was at the depot the day the girl arrived from the East. She looked frightened as any of them but was determined not to show it. Clyman saw her bags placed before her with an air of finality. She was small and neat and wore a gray, poplin gown trimmed with blue ribbon, and a little feathered jockey cap on the side of her head. She kept waiting for someone to pick up her bags and escort her to a hotel, her chin going higher each minute.

Clyman was there to appraise horses. But he took pity on her and presented himself with his hat under his arm. "Jess Clyman, miss. Nevada City. I can get you a hotel room if you'd like. It'll be no trouble."

She brought her eyes coolly upon him. They were the gray of a smoke tree, purplish and fine, and he knew at once that she was a member of the only class on earth he was in awe of — the lady. Highborn men or lowborn he could handle, but women of the upper class he did not quite know how to take.

"Thank you," she said. "There'll be someone to help me in a moment."

He set the bags down, sufficiently disciplined by her gaze, which came up from below him but managed to look down upon him. "Sure," he said. "Somebody will be bound to, if you wait long enough."

He went back to the saloon, not quite angry. Women, he guessed, had to be careful when they traveled, but that young lady was going to wish she had accepted his offer before night fell. There wasn't a hotel room left in El Paso.

The second time he saw the girl was two hours later, just before dusk, a cold, sweeping wind hurling grit at her as she came along the sidewalk. He was back in El Sueco, sitting with two Mexican girls. He had never drunk with more than one girl at a time before and he felt like a roué. But they had fastened themselves upon him in the hope, at the most, of acquiring a well-heeled friend — at the least, of acquiring a few drinks.

The girl stopped when she saw him through the dirty windowpanes. She was staggering along, carrying her own bags. Chivalry was as foreign to the town as cold beer. Then she saw the girls with him and a look of confusion came to her eyes, and she turned and hurried on. Jess left some money on the table and followed her.

He caught her fifty feet away, where she had set the bags down to rest. Once more he approached with his hat under his arm. "Still Jess Clyman, miss," he said. "Still from Nevada City. And I can still get you a room."

She wanted to accept in utmost gratitude, he knew. But she was afraid of him and couldn't forget things she had heard about men who drank with saloon girls. "Really," she said, "there must . . . I haven't tried them all, yet. There's one more . . ."

Clyman put on his hat and raised the bags. "That one's full, too." He smiled. "The girls in there were after me. I wasn't after them. That's the way it is in this town. If you want this room . . ."

She raised her chin again. It was simply in her; she couldn't help it. "What makes you so sure you can find me a room? They told me at the depot there wasn't a room anywhere."

"I was going to give you my room. I'll catch a shakedown at the depot."

"Oh!" Her mouth was small and round and she looked as though she felt rather small herself. "Mister Clyman, you're very patient and very generous, and . . . and I'm very sorry. But I can't let you do it."

He caught one bag under his arm, held the second by the grip, and had his other hand free to escort her along the teeming walk. "I don't know what else you can do, unless you want to share a stall with a stage horse. It isn't much of a hotel, but it's the best in this place."

By the time they reached it, he knew a few things about her. Her name was Susan Shelby. She was from Alabama, and sounded it. Her father was American consul-general in Mexico City. She was on the way to join him. She wanted to know what chance there was of their ever going on; she was trying to reach San Diego to take a boat.

"Not much," he said. "But we'll work something out."

"I hope so. The war can't last long, but if it should . . ." She stopped abruptly.

He saw her settled and was granted permission to come back at seven to take her somewhere to eat where she wouldn't be poisoned by the food.

Two more stages came clattering in, one from the east, one from the west. That brought the total to thirteen packed into the big stage yard. There were some 100 or more horses and mules in the corrals and mighty little hay for them. Clyman saw the division superintendent stomping back and forth between stables and station, a man crucified by his problems. The drivers sat around, looking less important than usual. Going were the days when they could command $400 or $500 a month to drive a stage fifty miles a day. The time was ripe. The waiting game was over.

Division Superintendent Niscannon was barricaded behind his desk when Clyman entered. He came in unannounced and unwelcome. Niscannon was a bearish, sour-eyed man with putty-textured skin rutted with harsh lines. For two weeks nobody had brought him a word of good news. If anyone wanted to see him, it was about finding a room or borrowing ten dollars or demanding that the stages get moving. He made a growl around his cigar as the younger man came in.

"You can sleep in the barn, if you want, but as for borrowing any money . . ."

"It's a hell of a situation, isn't it?" Clyman sat on a rawhide-latticed chair, crossed his legs, and hung his hat on one boot toe.

Niscannon went back to mourning over waybills and express vouchers. Jess Clyman was silent. The superintendent pivoted on the chair suddenly and exploded: "Look! If you want to jaw, there's a dozen drivers sitting outside that door drawing pay for doing just that. But I've got worries. I've got more worries than any man in Texas. If there's anything I don't want to look at, it's a man without worries."

"Everybody's got worries. I was going to Houston, but I got sidetracked and stuck in this place. Isn't that a worry?"

Niscannon closed his eyes on the old, old story and went back to his papers.

"On top of that, I've got a peck basket full of gold. And that worries me."

206

Niscannon's bloodshot gaze came up. "Find yourself a girl. You won't have it to worry over long."

Jess shook his head. "I'm going to invest it. Don't this seem like the damnedest time to be buying stagecoaches?"

At last the stage man perceived that his visitor was deviously backing into a horse trade. The vising of his jaws ceased. "It sure does. What do you want with stagecoaches?"

"I'm speculating. I speculate that, if I take a string of Concords into Mexico, I can sell them high. They're practically legal tender in the capital. Naturally I'd have to get them cheap."

"Naturally." Niscannon leaned back and rolled a cigar between his hands. "Why tell me about it?"

"You've got thirteen stages in the yard, a hundred stage animals, and nothing to feed them. One of these days a couple of dozen Union or Confederate troopers are going to slope in, throw a handful of scrip at you, and take them away. How's that going to make you look with the company? If there still is one."

"How does it make every agent and section boss on the Oxbow look, the way they're throwing up their hands and dumping everything in my lap?"

Jess Clyman shrugged, rising. "Well, it was just an idea. But I thought if you could sell those coaches and some of the wagons and stock, they might figure they had a good man out here. Maybe you'd be one of the ones they moved north with the line."

Niscannon bounced up as Clyman put on his hat. "Sit down! Sit down! Clyman . . . by God, if you're joshing me . . ." But he quickly convinced himself Clyman was serious by peering into his face, and he pulled his chair around so that their knees were almost touching, and said: "All right. Let's talk turkey."

CHAPTER
TWO

When he left the office, Clyman walked the lighter for $9,500 in gold removed from his money belt. He did not know whether the stage man planned to abscond with it or turn it in to the company. It did not concern him. He had bills of sale on the coaches, ten wagons, and seventy-five horses and mules. He had been given the name of Hugh Donovan, 4th Division section boss, who would shake up a crew of drivers and hostlers.

Jess moved fast. He was anxious to scour the dust of El Paso in the Big River. The coaches were his worry now.

Hugh Donovan was another of El Sueco's partisans. Jess found him, by description, shooting pool with a sallow, spectacularly thin man. He watched Donovan sink the five ball, try for another, and presently pick up a glass of beer from the edge of the table. He drained half the beer. He belched. He was a very large man in a tawny buckskin shirt, dark pants, and high, wrinkled boots. A sombrero with two matches under the hatband hung between his shoulders by a thong. His hair was crisp and short, blond going gray, and his eyes were deep and blue, set wide under the hard bone ridge of his brow. He was about forty-five.

What Clyman liked about him was that he could play a decent game of pool in a time of general catastrophe. He made himself known to Donovan, and the big man sank a couple more and then came over to stand by Jess while the other man shot. "You say Niscannon sent you?"

"He thought you could help me find twenty-five men overnight. Thirteen stage drivers and a dozen others. Two of them ought to be good shots with a rifle, for meat-getters."

Jess saw him looking over in the mirror behind the bar. "What do you want with thirteen drivers?"

"You guess. I want them by tomorrow noon. I'm not trying to fool anybody about where we're going. It'll be Mexico City, if we're lucky, and I'll pay two hundred a month to the drivers, a hundred to the rest. They can take five hundred pounds of freight apiece to sell in the capital. Guns, tools . . . anything like that. They'll all make a killing."

The lean, hollow-chested man playing pool with Donovan looked around. "Did somebody say Mexico City?" He stood, leaning on his cue.

Donovan frowned. "Don't publish it, Doc. Clyman, this is Doc Bible. Maybe you'd like a sawbones along. Doc would give his right eye, the good one, to get out of this rat trap."

The doctor had a long, pinched countenance with a frazzled, light brown imperial on his chin. His left eye had a peculiar yellowish-green cast and the pupil was too large. Jess suddenly realized it was a makeshift, probably a lynx-eye from a taxidermist shop. It caused

210

him to smile as he shook Bible's hand, and Bible winked the other eye and said: "It's got all kinds of advantages. I'll hate to give it up if I ever get back to civilization. I can see in the dark with that one, you know. So you're going to Mexico . . . ?" He said it with the greatest relish and curiosity.

Donovan glanced about them. "Clyman, if you want to get out of town, I'd walk soft and move damn' quick. Let's go outside."

They left the saloon and walked in the plaza. A series of dingy alleys converged on the treeless square, where an endless procession of women and girls with *ollas* or wooden buckets balanced on their shoulders trudged to the stone well in the center of it. Bull teams jostled, horsemen seemed in a rush to go somewhere, although there was nowhere to go.

Doc Bible kept peering at Clyman. "I'd pay you double fare to get out of here, Clyman, even to Mexico. I could get a boat from Topolobampo to Frisco. What are you charging?"

"It isn't a common carrier proposition. Every passenger will make a hand. But you can go as company surgeon, and no charge."

The doctor grasped his hand. "I'll set you a broken leg or cure you a bellyache right now. Say the word."

Donovan's competent gaze was on the jam of dusty, crimson coaches in the stage yard. "Twenty-five men. I'll make a deal with you. Twenty-four . . . and myself." He grinned.

"Can you drive a stage?"

"No, but I can shoot an antelope as far as I can see one. If Niscannon's sold out, I've got no job to hold me. I'll pick up a load of junk jewelry and take over them brown-eyed women the way Cortez took Mexico."

Jess measured the section boss for an instant. The man's strengths were obvious enough — aggressiveness, confidence, leadership — but it was his weaknesses Clyman was interested in. These might be vanity and singleness of purpose that lapped over into stubbornness. "These men are all used to taking orders from you," he said. "Make it plain that they'll be taking orders from me on this trip."

Donovan looked at him steadily, his brown face flat. Then, grinning quickly, he struck him on the shoulder. "I'll have them call you commodore, if you say so."

With this done, the gun primed and ready to be fired, Jess thought again of Susan Shelby. He had only a faint notion that she'd be interested in a trip south. He wouldn't blame her. A delicately reared young woman, if she had any imagination, would faint at the thought of the hazards and inconveniences of such a trip. But he meant to ask her.

He put in the afternoon buying supplies and seeing them packed. Flour, salt, powder and ball, hardware. Everything you could not pick or shoot on the trail. He inspected the stagecoaches for cut spindles and sprung thorough braces. He met the drivers and got their hands, individually, that they would stay with the train as far as Mexico City. He set departure for ten o'clock the next morning.

212

At seven that evening he went down the hallway of the hotel through a faint blue of whale-oil smoke and the conglomerate body smell of too many people living too close together. He knocked at the door of Susan Shelby's room and waited. He waited fifteen minutes in the hall. Then he went to the noisy central room and listened to the racket of war talk and assorted complaints for another fifteen. At length she appeared.

She was unbelievably trim; she was contrite and vivacious at one time. She wore the same gray gown with its touches of blue, but she had managed to get every travel wrinkle out of it, and the dark-brown sausage ringlets at the back of her head were neat and shining as metal turnings. She looked to Jess like something that ought to be under a glass bell to keep off the dust. She could have been two hours late and carried it off as well.

"I had so many things to do," she told him, "and then I slept . . . and then you knocked at the door. You don't know how fast I dressed."

Jess guided her through the raucous traffic of the sidewalk. She seemed to flinch from hurrying Mexicans. He led her past the stage depot where, for the first night in two weeks, the superintendent's office was dark. Niscannon would sleep for a week. Jess had had the coaches aligned, ready for teaming, and they bulked, freshly washed, in a gleaming dark line within the gate. He held the girl there a moment.

"How do they look to you?"

She shuddered. "I know how a pullet feels in a gunny sack, after coming all the way from Tipton in one of those things."

"Depends on what you're looking at. I'm looking at thirteen Concord stages, as saleable as ten-cent diamonds. I bought them today."

She turned her eyes up to his face in astonishment. "Jess! What do you want with them?"

"I'm going to sell them again."

"But where? Who else would be foolish enough to buy them?"

They came to the restaurant, and he pushed the door open on a dimly lighted scene of limber-legged tables and smoking lamps. At a tile stove in the rear a fat Mexican woman was dipping tortillas in grease, sprinkling ground cheese and onions on them, and dousing the roll with earth-red chili. The old, familiar smell of Mexican cooking was as heart-warming to him as the sound of a sweetheart's voice. But he had to urge Susan Shelby into the room with a promise.

"It tastes better than it looks."

He ordered, aware that she wasn't going to like it. On the other hand, the food was safer than spoiled beef in an American café. She had a little difficulty getting back to the coaches again. "I still don't see how you expect . . ."

"I don't. Not here. I'm taking them south."

"But there's nothing south of here but Mexico."

"That's right, Mexico City."

She caught her breath, started to say something, and then frowned and looked down at the table. The food

214

came, two plates smoking with Mexican rice, *frijoles,* *huevos rancheros*, and *enchiladas*. Susan pushed at the *enchilada* with an iron fork. She took a little and looked at him in distress. She got it down and her eyes flooded with tears. It was incandescent with chili, which was the beauty of it. Finally she ate the rice and eggs and drank the coffee.

"Mexico City," she mused. "Did you know that was where I was going when I was put off here?"

"You told me. You said your father was American consul."

"Confederate American consul."

She said it with pride, her eyes challenging him. He scowled. Politics did not excite him, and the war still seemed to be none of his business. He side-stepped a discussion of it.

"It isn't much of a road. I've got a map, but I think a lot of it's just a cow track. But what I was thinking, if you really want to get there . . ."

She sat with eyes beginning to lighten, waiting for him to say it. Something slowed her down. If this were another third-rate café he was asking her into, he didn't want to be held responsible. "I make no promises or predictions. But if you want to go along, you'll have your own coach and it won't cost you anything."

"It frightens me, but it frightens me still worse to think of staying here. Jess, it's fine of you to ask me. I'd like to go."

All the way back to the hotel he felt the lift of being with her. Yet there was a shading of intuition about it when he thought of the weeks ahead. She would have

215

no maid, no pampering, her remembrances of the Oxbow would seem like a dream. Jess Clyman hoped she could take it.

At her door he said: "Ten o'clock. Get all the sleep you can. We'll travel fast the first couple of days."

And then, because she was the prettiest woman he had seen since he left San Francisco, and because she was provoking him with her eyes, he took her shoulders gently in his hands, bent, and kissed her on the lips. She repulsed him without moving or speaking. It was like kissing a picture. She regarded him coolly.

"Have I paid my fare, now? Or will there be other installments?" She said that very slowly.

Jess said: "You're paid up. You were before. Good night." He was not so much contrite as angry and he didn't understand why.

Niscannon had said he could spend the night in the stage station, in a back room loaded with crated files and a cot. Dr. Bible was sleeping in one of the coaches, glad to be shut of a louse-ridden hotel room on the river. There was a barracks-like building at the rear of the stage corral where the drivers and hostlers bunked. Jess sat up late, studying his maps. He had the creeping fears of any man going into a dangerous gamble, not quite ready to back out, not eager to push ahead. It was after twelve when he snuffed the lamp and pulled off boots and shirt.

He was sitting on the cot, rolling a last cigarette, when he saw a light reflected on the wall. He glanced through the window. He saw only the dark corral with its throng of horses, and beyond it the low, pole-beamed façade of the employees' quarters. A wash of light ruddied the tawny adobe wall, reflecting faintly into Jess's room. He could not see the source of it. It was to the left, toward the stage barn. He saw the horses begin to move restlessly and all at once it struck at him.

He tugged at his boots, pulled his carbine from the head of the cot, and strode through the dark freight room to the side door. He opened it and stood there for a moment. His impulse to action ran down. Looking through it was like stirring up the lees of a nightmare.

Two coaches were already beginning to burn, and the man who set fire to the second was climbing a wheel hub of the third with a coach lamp in his hand, the brass lens housing removed and the wick turned up high. A second man, four coaches ahead of him, pulled a lamp from its socket, drew the stopper, and dumped the whale oil onto the floor beneath the driver's seat. Then he ducked on to the next in the compact line of coaches.

Jess pushed open the cheesecloth-frame screen door. A rusty spring squawked. Both men turned in alarm. Clyman set the stock of the gun to his shoulder and leaned against the jamb. He took aim at the man leaping from the wheel to the ground. The gun kick jolted him. The roar of the gun hit a dozen adobe walls and came rolling back at him in a cascade of sound. The hatless man with the lamp dropped it and lunged into the yard, reeled aside, and fell across the tongue.

Jess saw the other man draw a revolver, balance there with his boot on the hub of a front wheel, clutching the brake with his left hand while he threw down on the doorway. Ducking back, Clyman heard the expanding report of the gun; the door frame was hit and wrenched from one hinge. He struck it open again and saw the gunman rushing toward the gate. Clyman's gun was a six-shot Dragoon Colt with a shoulder stock and a long barrel. He squinted at the indistinct, running figure through the sights, took his shot, and knew at once he had missed.

Then there was another man in the gate. The running figure swerved, came up against the door of the baggage room, half raising his Colt. Jess heard him say in a gasp: "Hugh!"

Hugh Donovan, a tapered wedge against the faint luster of the town, stood with one foot a little ahead of the other, his left arm hanging, his right slightly hitched back. A gun flashed. The bullet, crossing only twenty feet of ground, hit the man hard, nailing him to the door. He staggered two steps away and went to his knees. Then he went forward on his face.

CHAPTER
THREE

Clyman lost the first stage. He saved the second. When they were through fighting the fire, he went to the baggage room where Bible was tending the wounded men. The man Donovan had shot was killed instantly. The other was still alive, hanging to a thread of breath that sucked through the ragged wound in his chest. The bullet had driven a splinter of bone into his lung. Bible didn't expect him to live through the night. The man's name was Rice. He'd been one of the wagon drivers Donovan picked. The dead man's name was Naylor. Donovan stood with Clyman in the yard and swore.

"The dairty sons of Satan! Slave men they were, forever chattering about states' rights and low tariff and a parcel of other things I don't give a damn for one way or another. But I didn't see where it could matter what color a man's politics were, for this trip. They figgered, you see, there wouldn't be a trip. Maybe they thought you were taking these coaches north."

"Where would they get that notion?"

Donovan tugged at a shaggy blond eyebrow. "I don't know. Being you're a Californian, maybe." He scowled at the throng of drivers and hostlers about the door of the baggage room. "I'll be shakin' a few bushes tonight for any more Johnnies in this crew. Get your rest, Clyman. I'll sit up with them Concords myself."

But Jess didn't rest the balance of that night. A hex had been put on the trip. He wasn't superstitious but it bothered him to put his foot into a room that had been quarantined.

Nevertheless, he went ahead in the morning with as much confidence as he could display. He checked everything himself, assigned drivers to coaches, and inspected the loads of merchandise they were taking. He saw the teams watered and grained and, at ten, gave the word to hitch. Then he hurried to the hotel. He wanted to get out of town before all the frightened travelers who inhabited it realized a train was going out. Clubs couldn't beat them off if they discovered it.

Susan Shelby called through the door that she'd be right out. Twenty minutes later she appeared. Jess seized the bags and hurried her out without listening to her excuses. She was, he decided, one of those women born with their clocks set back an hour.

Someone had shut the gate of the stage yard. Before it a shouting mob surged. Men with suitcases, women with children, all trying to get through the cottonwood-pole gate to storm the crimson coaches stirring restlessly under four-horse teams. Jess pulled Susan Shelby aside. There was a door into the depot. He rapped until Niscannon opened it. Niscannon was still half drunk as a result of a celebration the night before. He bowed low to the girl and barred the door after them. He said: "Ye're a fool, Clyman, if you don't accept passengers at two hundred dollars a head."

"I'd be a fool if I did. I may make it if I travel light."

He rushed Susan into the yard. The driver of her coach was already on the box, a big, iron-mustached man named Ben Dallas. He was taking along a load of black silk bolt cloth that he thought he could sell to women in mourning, which in Mexico included anyone over two. Jess put Susan in and hesitated with his hand on the latch.

"Still sure?"

Her color was that of muslin but she smiled: "Sure, Jess."

Clyman slung up onto the box of the lead coach. The driver sat flicking his whip at pebbles. He was a leathery old-timer named Gil Applegate. He wore a collar-band shirt with no collar, a wadded silk vest much stained with food, and buckskin pants. He glanced at Jess through the round, silver spectacles he wore. "Know this is a crazy idear, don't you?"

"If it's too crazy, you don't have to go along."

Applegate spat tobacco juice on a wheeler's rump. He picked up a copper bugle from under the seat, decorated with a silk tassel, and wiped his lips. "As long as we've got Hortencia along, you don't have to worry. Roll 'em?"

Jess signaled the gate men to open it. "Roll 'em."

Applegate blew a sour little flourish that was his trademark. Other drivers sounded their calls, a brassy tangle of discord that somehow threaded a ramrod down a man's spine. The gate swung in.

There was a wild rush of would-be passengers into the yard. Men grabbed at the harness bags and

221

pounded on the panels. Applegate kicked off the brake and let the buckskin cracker of his whip singe a man's ear. The coach rolled forward with a grind of iron tires.

Jess heard a woman's shriek: "Murderers!" He saw a man hold up a chamois bag and shout: "A thousand dollars!" He had to discipline himself, to recall with loaded coaches on a trip like this he could hope for nothing but disaster. He could not feed them, bunk them, nor tend the inevitable sick. He looked straight ahead and the team reared and lunged out onto the plaza. He stood up to look behind. The other stages were in motion, thrusting through the mob. Then they were out of his vision as Applegate hawed the team into the alley beside the station and let it run. There was a crowded vista of adobes boxing in a pot-holed street, then a glimpse of open land and cottonwoods along the river, and finally they were on the river road, clattering along toward the ford, with the midnight-blue mountains of Mexico beyond the desert.

There was a desolate little store and *cantina* a few miles below the border, where border guards and riff-raff made occasional stops for food and drink. Clyman stopped here and treated himself to a mescal while the others, except Applegate, waited outside. He talked to the proprietor, a fat *mestizo* named Corrales.

He bought Corrales four drinks, and then backed into his subject. He was taking a train of stagecoaches to *la capital* for the Mexican government. Which government? Ah, the revolutionary government of

Juárez. He wondered what he could hope for on the trail.

Corrales fished a fly from his drink with a fat forefinger. "Only the *indios, capitán,* and the *reaccionarios,* and, of course, the *bandidos.* I know of no soldiers this far north, though in Sinaloa . . ." He shrugged. "But there is a gentle murderer by the name of Jesús Calzadillos in Chihuahua. He might have been here last week. How should I know? He has not the money for uniforms for his men, so he is still a *bandido.* He knows many tricks with ants and honey."

Jess stacked fifty *pesos* on the counter. "We know a few with rifles. But if you see him, tell him we were heading for Hermosillo, eh?"

They rolled steadily through the day, coming at sundown to the shore of Lago de Los Patos. Clouds of ducks and cranes rose at their approach; some of the men had loaded with birdshot and enough were brought down for several meals. They were on a dark plain reaching distantly to the east and running up against a chain of mountains a few miles to the west. Wild hay, green and young-tasselled, rustled hub high to the coaches. The teamsters were to draw extra pay as stock handlers. They watered the horses and mules, grained them, and two of the men saddled to guard the herd through the night.

The wagons and coaches were drawn up in a circle, with the supper fires inside. Ben Dallas had appointed himself caretaker of the Shelby girl. He brought a leather seat cushion for her to sit on at dinner. He carried her a tin plate heaped with fried meat and potatoes. Jess bottled his scowls until the conversation came around to the war.

Dallas said: "Miss Shelby tells me it's a crime what them Yankees have already done in Kentucky. A disgrace. Farms pillaged with the crops just coming through the ground! Women and kids killed and . . ."

"So I hear tell," said Donovan seriously.

Applegate squinted at a cube of steak on his fork. "I heerd just the reverse. I heerd the Johnnies had raided into Ohio and burned a town clear to the ground."

Dallas leveled a finger at him. "Now that," he said, "is a damned . . . excuse me, miss . . . an everlastin' lie."

Jess came in sharply: "We're going to have a house rule on this trip. Anybody that talks politics gets his tongue hauled out by the roots. There's only one thing has caused more trouble than women, and that's politics."

The firelight had its sparks in Susan's eyes. "You don't approve of the South, Mister Clyman?"

"I didn't say that. I said I don't approve of wrangling over things nobody knows anything about."

"I know something about the South. My father . . ."

"I know. If I wanted to know about the South, I'd ask a Northerner. If I wanted to know about the North, I'd ask you. Then I'd figure both were telling ten percent of the truth, and I still wouldn't know anything."

He saw the watchful faces about the fire studying him. A throb of anxiety woke in him. He had suddenly the feeling that he was talking to a jury, that the things he said might come back at him from a prosecutor's mouth. He heard Hugh Donovan state: "You must have some feelings about it. It's pretty big."

"It's too big to decide in thirty days. When it comes to things like that, I like to grind on them a while before I make up my mind. I wish more politicians were that way. But the one thing I can tell you is that we're out here to drive some stages fifteen hundred miles south. We'll have Indians to fight, *bandidos*, and, like as not, fevers. But if I can help it, we aren't going to fight each other."

Dr. Bible nodded, glints of humor in his eyes, his long face gouged by light and shadow. "Spoken like a statesman. I'll be glad to perform that operation you spoke of, Clyman, on the first man who talks politics."

"Or woman?" the Shelby girl put in tartly.

Bible smiled. "A pretty woman has certain rights, one of which is not to turn a man's words back upon him."

Susan finished her dinner quickly and rose to go to her coach. Dallas started to get to his feet to escort her, but Jess put a hand on the man's shoulder. "My monuments are built and my claim recorded," he said softly.

Dallas's broad, heavy-browed face watched him a moment, and then turned away. Jess walked after her. He took her arm as they went through the grass. "Sue, I'm sorry. I'm on neither side. But politics could split this train right up the middle."

"Politics have split the country. Is your train more important than your country?"

"That," Jess said, "is one of the prettiest pieces of feminine logic I have ever heard. I have an idea, if I were to put that question to you ten days from now, you'd say the train was more important even than whether Alabama keeps her slaves or turns them loose." He saw the white anger coming into her face. He gripped both her hands. "I said I was sorry. Let's leave it like that."

She turned away without a word and mounted the step of her coach.

CHAPTER
FOUR

In the middle of the night a shot split the prairie with a clean, echoless, spiteful *crack*. Jess, sleeping under the stage, rolled out of his blankets and began pulling on britches and boots, swearing. The sound wasn't close, but it was followed immediately by the soft rush of horses' hoofs. Applegate was raising a profane clatter atop the coach. They heard the racket of horses falling and squealing; they were hobbled to make herding easier and seemed to be falling all over themselves in the attempt to run.

There came another shot, and a cry. Jess swerved around the rear of the coach and found his pony loosely saddled. He fumbled with the latigo, hearing Dr. Bible shouting: "Clyman! What in hell?"

"Horse raid!" Jess yelled.

Only six men had saddles, although there were saddle horses among the wagon stock that had been kept in the circle for emergencies. He mounted and rode over to where Bible, Applegate, Ben Dallas, and three hostlers were saddling. For a moment his impulse was to order them onto a firing line beneath the stages: this could be a raid by *bandidos*, revolutionaries, or Indians. It was not likely a small raiding party, but in any case it would merely be slow death to be marooned without stock.

The horses were making so much noise, about a quarter mile west, that it was no trick to follow. Leading out, Clyman found the dark bulk of the herd. He pulled in. The others ranged in beside him. He told Applegate and Dallas to cut north around the tail of the herd and sent three others against the flank.

Then they heard a horseman hammering down out of the darkness to the north. The men deployed while Jess waited. The man pulled in short of him and apparently was endeavoring to find the riders he had heard. Clyman recognized the stringy shape of Toll Breckwalter, one of the night guards. He called to him, and rode forward.

Breckwalter was winded and his voice was high and stretched. "They knocked Ashley over. There was only a couple of them, it sounded like. I think the horses are just boogered."

They rode out and found the horses slowing, beginning to scatter. There was no indication of raiders. Jess left four men to gather the herd, and then rode back to find Sam Ashley.

They came in with Ashley twenty minutes later. The fire had been built up, water was heating, and Dr. Bible spread a blanket to the ground and motioned the men to lay the wounded man on it. He worked without much sureness, it seemed to Jess, and the smell about him was not of disinfectants but of whiskey. Bible brought a mashed lead ball from the man's hip with tweezers. While he was cleaning the wound of the now-rousing patient, he pulled out a bit of wadding. He dropped it in the granite washbasin. Something about it caused Jess to pull it out on a matchstick to examine it.

He grunted and dropped it into the fire. It was the paper patch that had been wrapped about the ball. Evidently the gunman had fumbled in loading the patch, and torn a bit of paper off something in his pocket to replace it. What he had wrapped about the ball was the corner of an American dollar bill.

Hugh Donovan came in a few minutes later. His horse had been worked hard and he threw a blanket over it before he joined the others at the fire.

Jess asked: "Where were you? Did they run you off, too?"

The firelight stroked the hard planes of Donovan's face. "I heard the horses moving before it happened. I didn't see any call to turn the camp inside out. I went out to see."

"Two jaspers sloping for the mountains, after the shot. They got Sam."

Staring into the fire as he sat cross-legged, Bible muttered: "He may live the night. He won't live the week." No one commented, and the lanky physician, with his gray-green cat's eye glinting, stared around the circle.

The party broke up. Applegate was grunting as he tried to make himself comfortable on his straw shakedown. Jess climbed to the box and reached under the seat. He kept his maps there, and suddenly too many things pointed to the fact that they might be as important to someone else as they were to him. He grubbed deeper among the tools and odds and ends: the long roll was gone.

Applegate heard him curse. "Now what?"

Jess sat on the seat, gazing into the darkness. Finally he turned. "Applegate, how do your politics run?"

The driver lay on his belly on the deck to stare at him. "You ain't going to start a political argument with me, now?"

"Not if you're Union. Otherwise, keep still."

"I'm from Pennsylvania. Going back one day and likely join up."

"My plans, too, only I'm for California where I come from. Gil, the maps are gone."

Applegate groaned. "Maybe they shook out. We can ride back."

"No. Somebody took them tonight because I was tracing tomorrow's travel after dinner."

"You know how to git them back, don't you? Shake down every man in camp and shoot the son-of-a-bitch."

". . . There's a better way. We aren't lost because I've got a small duplicate in my boot. I think they'll be brought back if we keep still. Gil" — he sighed — "this is a misbegotten outfit if ever there was one. A doctor that's turnin' into a drunk, a girl that's too pretty and Southern for anybody's good . . . and a traitor in camp."

Applegate's cheap vulcanite plates rattled hollowly. "How do you know that?"

"Sam Ashley was shot by somebody in camp. The bullet that shot him carried a paper-patch torn off an

American bill. Would Indians or *bandidos* be heeled with American money? They couldn't spend it."

They both looked down at the sleeping circle of the camp with its surging red heart of dying coals. Applegate asked slowly: "Who do you reckon . . . ?"

"I think I can find out. But I can't go to shooting my mouth off too quick because he might have friends. He may have about twenty friends and nobody but you and me for enemies. We may know within forty-eight hours. We'll hit the cut-off to Texas at El Venado. It's marked on the map. If anybody else wants these stages of mine, I don't think he'll want to travel any deeper than that."

The morning was as many mornings would be before they reached Mexico City. Lame stock to tend, feed to dole out, running gear to tar. When Jess gave the order to stretch out, Applegate remarked dryly: "They're back now."

"Did you see who returned them?"

Applegate let the lines slip through his fingers, adjusting them. "Yup."

"The girl?"

Applegate glanced at him. "You don't seem surprised."

"I'd have been surprised if whoever wanted them had the guts to do it himself."

He didn't let his emotions get into his voice but he couldn't keep them out of his head. It made him want to punish her before anyone. She was a damned brainless little tramp, a cat's-paw that didn't stop to look at end results when she went into a thing. But she was a lovely tramp, and she had her fingers on the strings that governed his life in a disturbing way. But if he had to sleep with every *chamaca* in every pueblo they passed, he wouldn't let her know she meant any more to him than she had when they left.

Through a morning of almost summer warmth, they wound deeper into the vast cattle empire of Chihuahua. Sam Ashley died without regaining consciousness; they buried him beside the road.

The stage trail to Chihuahua City was a deep trough in the tall grass along the base of the Blue Mountains. If it continued in as good condition, they would make the city in five days. They would reach El Venado, and the junction of the Texas trail, by the following evening.

Jess Clyman's gaze ranged continually along the foothills. These Tarahumare Indians were rough; Jesús Calzadillos, the *bandido* who aspired to be a general, might be even rougher. He could trade coaches for money, uniforms, weapons. A picket-like line of trees made a dark piping on the mountain-locked prairie ahead of them. Río Tula cut its sharp scallops among the trees and emptied into a muddy seep far to the east. Jess and Donovan rode ahead to scout the trees before bringing the coaches on. It was safe, and Donovan lingered to study the land up west, toward the hills.

"I seen antelope rumps up there, Jess. We'd better git 'em whilst we can."

He looked back for approval, and found Jess's eyes on him in level, unfriendly scrutiny. Jess said: "You've got plenty of plans but not quite enough guts to shove them through."

Donovan stirred on the saddle. He cleared his throat. "What's got into you, Jess?"

"Too many killings. You sicced Naylor onto the coaches, and then shot him. You killed Sam Ashley last night. Let me have your poke." His revolver came out with smooth, disarming speed.

Donovan's brows pulled. "A detective one minute, a highwayman the next."

"Let's see your poke!"

The stage man pulled a chamois bag with a clasp top from his hip pocket. He tossed it to Jess. Jess heard the dull *clink* of coins as he caught it. He opened it and pulled out a roll of bills that lay on top. He peeled off the top one and found a torn corner. He put the rest of the money back into the purse and tossed it to Donovan.

"Still a detective. Doc Bible pulled the other part of this bill out of Ashley's wound. What's your game?"

Donovan pocketed the leather poke, and drew one boot from the stirrup and put his leg across the saddle swell. "You've got a lot of ideas. What's your idea about this?"

"Either you're a transplanted Copperhead, or you think you ought to have the stages instead of me. Which is it?"

Donovan's mouth smiled. "Do either of these notions jibe with trying to burn the coaches?"

Jess had not yet reconciled it himself. He shook his head. "But I'll swear you had a finger in it."

Donovan smiled. "In a way, Rice and Naylor were good men, but crazy as hoot owls. I told them you were

233

taking the coaches to Mexico to ship to California for the northern supply route. The same as I told them all. That was just to bring them along, but the damned fools got patriotic fever and decided to burn them before we left. Well, a burned stagecoach is no good to anybody, and I'm glad I came along in time to help you clean 'em out."

"What about the stock raid last night?"

Donovan wiped his mouth. "The sooner I can stall you, the better I'll like it. This is a harebrained idea of going to Mexico. You'll never make it. But I figure a man could cache these Concords down near Laredo and make a deal with the julep-merchants. In fact, now that you're in on it, I'll split with you."

Jess laughed briefly. "You can look down the barrel of a gun and make an offer like that!"

Donovan shook his head. "You ain't going to kill me, Jess. You can't afford to. The boys would lynch you. They're mine, every damn' one of them! Even the girl. Not counting the sawbones and Applegate, of course. What are you going to do about it?" He didn't give Jess long to reply. He said: "Jess, there ain't nothing you can do about it. You came out with your guard down. I'm giving you your chance. Take off right now and keep your health."

Jess grunted and put his Colt away. "You're a pretty good chess player but you want to look in back of you as well as in front. If you took these coaches, you wouldn't dare go back to El Paso. They may be fighting there already. And you'll find getting to Laredo is more than tracing the route on a map stolen by an empty-headed little tart. Remember these greasers down here were trained to kill Yankees only ten years ago. A lot of them still make it a hobby. Donovan, if you got to the border, I'd be as wrong as a man ever was. You'd ask about the next water hole and they'd direct you to a salt sink. You'd try to shake out of them which Indians to trust and which not to, and they'd lie and then send somebody to let them start their dance. You're a hell of a fine schemer, except that you forgot something. You're in a foreign country that would still be at war with us if it had the money."

Donovan's broad, brown face with its tough brows received it impassively. "I wasn't brought up in a ladies' seminary. I'll take on any fifty you can pick."

Jess laughed in his face. "You're a good barracks fighter, but your guts will turn to water in the field. The Mexicans have a song that goes . . . 'For zarapes, Saltillo. For soldiers, Chihuahua. For women, Jalisco . . . ' This is Chihuahua. Every peasant picking sap out of a cactus dreams of being a soldier, and, if you go along the way you think you will, a few of them are going to put their heads together and start an army."

Donovan's eyes scoffed. "What makes you better at getting through than I am?"

"Because I know them. And I've got letters. When I get into the danger zone, I'll hire guides on the strength of my letters." He shook his head, smiling confidently. "I'd hang you for killing Ashley, except for one thing. The boys might hang me. So we seem to be stalemated. You can't do without me, and I can't get rid of you . . .

yet. We'd better try a few more moves until one of us thinks of a way to clip the other."

He turned his pony and rode back, showing Donovan the broad target of his back . . .

CHAPTER
FIVE

Reaching the train, Jess tied his pony on behind and climbed up beside Applegate. Gil took the Concord through the bright, splashing little river. Donovan was out of sight, having gone after the antelope. And this was a tribute to Jess's dialectics, for about fifty percent of what he had given the stage man was fancy. Donovan had him in the tightest spot a man ever squeezed into. How many of the wagoners Donovan owned, Jess couldn't guess. He hadn't owned Ashley, that was obvious. And he didn't own Gil Applegate. But Ashley was dead, and Applegate and he made only two against twenty-four.

Jess looked back over the train. Susan Shelby, riding the box beside Ben Dallas as he brought the coach through the water, was leaning out to look at the stream. She appeared warm and uncomfortable in her heavy traveling dress. Suddenly she looked up at Jess.

"Mister Clyman, will we hit another stream tonight?"

"Not for two days."

"Then I'm going to ask you to wait up ahead a few minutes while I bathe. I haven't been so warm and dusty since I left the Oxbow."

"Go right ahead. The boys will enjoy it."

Some of the men chuckled. Susan put her chin up as color flooded her face. "Please stop and let me down," she said to Dallas. Dallas handed the team in. She closed her parasol with a snap. "You can go along for a mile or so and someone can come back after me." Imperiousness was out of place in someone six inches shorter than anyone else in the party.

Jess smiled. "You aren't afraid of the Indians or Calzadillos?"

"Not if you don't go far off and leave me."

"I ought to. There's an old saying about an eye for an eye. Do you understand?"

She saw the double meaning and her lips parted. Before she could reply, Jess sent the cavalcade forward with a down sweep of his arm. He signaled Dallas to drop the saddle horse trailing his coach. He glanced back a few minutes later and she was not in sight, but a white petticoat lay across a bush.

Everyone seemed to think it a good joke, except Dallas. The big driver drove in somber displeasure. Finally he pulled out a silver pocket watch.

"Fifteen minutes," he said. "Dammit, Clyman, you'd ought to know better than that. There's danger of Indians, and in the second place she ain't dressed to fork a saddle."

"It was her idea. It'll do her good."

Dallas's eyes combed the back country. He turned on the seat. "I'm going back for her."

Jess dropped down and went to seize the leader's tug. "You're going to keep right on, mister."

Dallas stood up. "Leave holt of that tug."

238

"Swing them horses back in line and keep moving," Jess snapped.

He released the trace, but, as he did so, Dallas brought the horses around. Jess swerved to catch the tug. Dallas, still on his feet, sent the thirty-foot whip out in a savage cast. The cracker caught Jess on the side of the neck. The pain was swift and disarming; he felt blood seeping down into his shirt. Dallas gave the whip to the horses on his next throw and they went lunging past the pony. Jess shook his head to clear it. Then he ran to untie his horse, mounted, and started after him. Dallas had turned the horses loose. They were trying to climb through the collars; the coach rocked like a baby buggy on the uneven ground.

Crossing behind it, Jess loped up the off side, holding his pace until he could lean over and close his hands on the side rail across the seat from Dallas. He left the saddle like a bull-dogger taking his ox, finding the floor with one boot and hauling himself up beside the driver. Dallas took a swift dally of the lines about the brake and, twisting on the seat, fired a looping overhand blow at Jess's chin. Jess took it on the shoulder, but it had the shocking power of a sledge.

Wild-eyed, Dallas lunged after him. Jess, slamming his punches aside, cuffed him on the ear. Dallas shook his head and scowled. He was a hand-pegged sort of man with the virility and homeliness of the country. He would not be taken to pieces by a few blows any more than a homemade saloon counter would collapse under a drunkard's fist. Jess's knuckles ached with a follow-up blow to the driver's forehead, but Dallas kept soberly about his business of pawing for a hold and clubbing with a fist like a bung starter. He hammered the meaty edge of that fist into the muscle at the base of Clyman's neck. It locked him in an aching paralysis. Jess had to let his right arm hang and jab with his left. Dallas circled both arms about his neck, locked them with a fist clamped on his own wrist, and hauled Jess's head down. His knee drove up. Jess took it on the cheek bone. Staggered, he reached up and got both hands on Dallas's windpipe. He had the sense to hang on while the driver clawed at his face; a man forgot everything when his breathing was tampered with.

Jess hung on like a badger. Now the hands mauling over his mouth and eyes seemed to push more than to gouge. He got an urgent note into the snorting gasps he managed to force past the blockade of Jess's thumbs. Something was off-key. Dallas was not fighting. He was floundering.

Jess stared at him. The driver's eyes were focused beyond the stage, off on the prairie. Involuntarily Jess relaxed. Dallas gasped: "¡Bandidos! Bandits, by God!"

Out of a foothill barranca, two miles west of the stalled wagon train, lurched a winding string of horsemen. They were crossing rim rock, but making time. They wore the white pants and shirts of peasants. The sun struck blue glints from their rifles.

Catastrophe has a fascination, a beauty and balance, and Jess stood there an instant almost in admiration of it. A quarter mile south were the wagons. A mile north was Susan Shelby, washing her body. There were at least forty bandits. Jess counted twenty-five in his outfit. Susan was in this spot despite his advice, but a woman was a woman, and — damn it! — had to be protected.

A single shot cracked, and the echoes poured down from the foothills. He saw a rider lope out of a brush thicket ahead of the outlaws and pound toward the caches and wagons waiting in a line as neat as a family of ducks on a pond. Applegate yelled something and hawed his team around to outline the circle.

The pony was back where Jess had left it. He shouted at Dallas. "Pull 'em in! Let me off. You go get the girl. Blow your bugle and give her time to start dressing. If she gets stubborn, come in without her. They may not find her."

Dallas was unable to stop the wild run of the team. He swung them and headed back toward Clyman's horse while they cooled off. They came out of their headlong run, and Jess jumped. He seized the reins and made the saddle without touching a stirrup.

The grass was so deep a horse could run safely only on the road ruts, gouged by carts and the stagecoaches. This was an advantage over the raiders, and God knew he needed one. He glanced back as he knifed into the circle just closing up. Dallas had reached the river and someone in a white undergarment was climbing into the coach.

Donovan racked in about a mile ahead of the Mexicans. They were jogging in a switch-backing line down a rocky slope to the grass. They held their guns shoulder-high with one arm and manipulated the reins of the other, as if only this device could retain the horses' balance. Applegate and the others were cutting the horses off the poles and slapping hobbles onto them. Jess yelled at them to throw and tie the horses as well. He wanted neither to stage a battle with seventy-five crazy broncos stampeding around, nor to have them shot.

Most of the men had seen Indians in action at some time or other, but there was no assurance that Mexicans would attack in the same fashion. Certainly not if they had any sense, for they didn't outnumber the wagoners sufficiently to take the risks of circling. Applegate said the only way was to lie under the coaches and wait. But when some of the men tried it, they found the grass was so high they couldn't get a shot to the bandits until they were close enough to strike straight through into the hasty stockade.

This gave Jess an idea. Measuring, he saw Calzadillos's men hitting the grass and letting their jughead ponies romp down across the flats. Less than a half mile to go, now. But Ben Dallas, standing on the box with both arms extended across the clattering void between the dashboard and the wheelers' rumps, was bringing the Concord in at a full run. They had left a slot for him, and he rammed the coach into it and others piled onto the team and ripped the snaps loose.

Jess had to fire a shot before anyone tamed down enough to listen to him. "Five of you take positions on top of the coaches. The rest of us are going out into the grass. Donovan, you pick ten and I'll take the rest. Crawl about a hundred feet out. Stay down until you've

242

got a sure shot. I figure they'll pull up about there to start peppering."

He looked around, taking a quick inventory. The horses were down with a couple of men to watch them. Donovan was tolling off his men. Applegate was jamming an extra Colt under his belt, and at the window of Dallas's coach Susan Shelby's face showed whitely. Dr. Bible stood with a long horse pistol hanging from his fingers.

They crawled under the wagons and out into the grass. It was tender and moist and fragrant; it absorbed the sound of the running horses almost completely. Yet before he had crawled fifty feet, Jess heard the yells start: *"¡A bajo los Yanquis! ¡A bajo los Tejanos!"*

He couldn't see the others. He hoped Calzadillos could not, either. A light desert breeze stroked the grass. His hands sweatily clenched the Dragoon pistol, the off-breed .44 with the barrel of a revolver, and the stock and firepower of a repeating rifle. He waited until his nerves were pulled out to a plucked tautness. His body throbbed to the hammer blows of hoofs on the earth. He heard the men on the Concords begin to fire and a voice shouted something in Spanish so close he could hear the breathiness of it: *"¡Bajen ustedes!"* Dismount! Jess ripped out a Rebel yell and came to his knees. The peasant army, uniformed in the garb of poverty, carrying weapons out of style for twenty years, was scrambling out of the high trees. There was an Oriental cast to the faces Jess saw, the eyes narrow and wispy, with lip and chin beards marking most of them. He picked out a hatless outlaw who wore a

243

red-and-gray poncho for his target. The man was about forty feet away. He put a shot into the outlaw's side as he left the saddle. Then he cocked the gun again and heard Gil Applegate's gun roar a few yards to his right. A second outlaw fell before he knew he had been fired at.

Heads were popping up all around, with every cheek against a gunstock. Gunfire crackled with the uneven tempo of popcorn explosions. There was hardly a chance for a man to miss at this range. Ponies and their riders threshed in the grass; bandits came up on their stirrups and were pitched from the saddle.

Back about fifty feet was a lean, hawk-faced Mexican with a conical sombrero crusted with silver and a horse carrying forty pounds of it on his bridle. This man fired a shot from his rifle, and suddenly wheeled and started back up the long slope to the foothills. As an afterthought he turned to shout: "*¡Haga a atrás!*" This merely made it official, as every *bandido* who was able to roll a spur was already falling back.

CHAPTER
SIX

There was powder and ball in the downed outlaws'
pouches, but the guns were cumbersome and rusty.
Jesús Calzadillos must wait many months before he
could call himself a general. He had left sixteen of his
men on the ground. Bible took care of the wounded,
and they left them covered with their own saddle
blankets. None of the Americans had taken a wound.

Darkness settled sootily over the prairie. There was
not a peasant's *jacal* to break the limitless dark with
a light, or a town to glow beyond a hill, nothing but
their three cook fires, shining, clean and clear, as stars
in the cold desert night. The men were exhausted with
the aftermath of the fight. They ate hungrily, chewing
poorly cooked duck, fried onions, and camp bread
burned on the bottom. Jess looked them over, trying to
catch some indication from each man's face or actions
as to how he stood — with him or against?

Susan did not look at him at all. Ben Dallas kept
forcing food on her, and her good nature was wearing
thin. He made a loutish, boastful lover of the
"feel-them-muscles" school.

Clyman made an offhand speech. "You've had your
baptism. They may keep on baptizing us all the way.

Things are apt to be tougher than I thought. The saloonkeeper at the border warned me that the Juáristas and the reactionaries are making trouble everywhere. It's a religious war, and there's nothing worse."

He saw Susan's eyes on him, dark and timid. He heard Breckwalter, partner of the man who had been killed the night before, say gruffly: "Anybody can start a thing. Not everybody can finish it."

Jess caught his eyes. "But nobody can finish it with a split crew." From his tin plate, Hugh Donovan's gaze rose slowly and with a dogged thrust. Donovan said nothing, but light ran fluidly along the browned barrel of his saddle gun lying across his lap. "Last night," Jess said, "somebody borrowed my maps. I got the impression he might be planning an excursion of his own. Maybe to Laredo. All I want to say now is that it's to that man's interest, and his friends', if he has any, to stick with the train. The Texas trail is suicide. Where we're going, we've got a chance. Make up your minds what you want. To die rich or to live well-heeled."

He went over to his own coach, stripped off his buckskin shirt, and hung a lamp in a window and a mirror against a trim poplar panel. He got out his shaving things and worked up a crisp lather. As he daubed it on his jaws, he saw Susan's reflection in the mirror. He didn't turn. She stood there a moment.

"I'm sorry, Jess."

"About what?"

That stopped her momentarily, and, when he looked down, she was obviously trying to decide what he knew, exactly. "About . . . making you let me bathe," she said.

"That's all right. It would have been your funeral if they'd found you before they'd found us."

She sat on the sill of the door. All the pride and petulance was out of her face tonight. "You don't like me, Jess, do you?"

The razor whispered along his jaw. "It's your friends I don't like."

She frowned. "Ben Dallas?"

"No. Hugh Donovan."

"Donovan is no particular friend of mine. I've hardly spoken to him since we left. What do you mean?"

"You aren't friendly enough with him to steal a roll of maps for him?"

He heard the quick drawing in of her breath. He turned with the razor loaded with lather peppered with stubble: suddenly he flicked it and the lather struck her on the mouth. "It was nice of you to bring them back. You'd make a dandy little spy, except that you haven't the sense to go with your lack of scruples."

She wiped the lather away, tears starting in her eyes. "I didn't do it for Donovan," she said falteringly. "I did it for myself. For what I believe in."

He laughed. "What do you believe in? Susan Shelby? That she should never go hungry, dirty, or unsatisfied?"

"I . . . I believe in the things the South stands for."

"What does it stand for?"

"For . . . for states' rights, and a low tariff, and . . ."

"One thing, I would never make a thief and a liar out of myself for a slogan. Those are the things they've told you. Are you sure enough about them to condemn

Applegate and me to death, and take a chance of being massacred on a lost trail yourself?"

Susan looked up at him, earnest but confused. "I didn't do any such thing! Mister Donovan told me you weren't taking these stages to Mexico to sell at all. That you were going to ship them to California to use against the Confederacy. I wanted to know. I thought you might have traced the route on the map . . ."

He examined her eyes and mouth, and all he could see was sincerity. Yet he remembered how stealthily she had stolen the maps, how completely selfish every act of hers that he had witnessed had been. He turned back to the mirror and placed the bright edge of the razor against a sideburn.

"I'm going to give you some advice. Get right with me or with Donovan damn' quick. We hit the Texas cut-off tomorrow, and it's just possible Donovan will call out the guard then. He can take nearly every man I've got. They may kill me, or they may just rob me. But whichever they do, they'll know they've been about the doing of it."

When everyone else had turned in, Clyman went out to inspect the stock, and returned in fifteen minutes, throwing his bedroll under the crimson coach and sliding into the blankets. He lay there about an hour, and then silently rolled out of them into the grass. He left the blankets tousled. He crawled about fifty feet and lay in the deep mat of wild grass. If an attack came, it would come with a shot at him.

248

He held to one fact. That Donovan had not had time before leaving El Paso to do a thorough job of hand-picking a crew. There must be some of the drivers with Northern leanings, or merely honest ones. Some men who might see through his pratings about the Confederacy to the fundamental fact that he was acting for the good of Hugh Donovan. These were the men Jess hoped he had reached with his campfire preachment.

It was damp and cold in the grass, and the fire sank to embers and the stars burnished themselves on the black velvet of the sky. Horses moved in the yonder distance, scuffing over rocks. Jess was barely able to see them, moving across a ridge. His heart thudded. They were moving faster than grazing horses moved. Then from the camp he heard sounds carefully muffled; a man dropped silently from a coach and went through the ring of Concords to step into the grass. Another appeared with a saddle over his shoulder. They came like shadows from all parts of the camp, filing out into the grass. Ten, eleven, twelve . . . They did not gather, but moved to a broken line toward the horse herd. There were sixteen of them, and Donovan's massive shape led the rest.

Jess did some calculations. Sixteen moving out meant eight left behind. Assume these eight were loyal. They were still outnumbered two to one. Jess could throw down on them, drop a couple, and be killed with the rest when Donovan marshaled his men.

They walked with hardly a sound in a straight line from the stages toward the mountains. The horses had disappeared over the ridge. There were left nine men, a girl, and twelve stagecoaches with nothing to pull them. As the deserters crossed the ridge, Jess got up and walked into camp. He went around and glanced at each man, his Colt in his hand. They were sleeping, not lying there waiting for a signal to kill the dubious ones. Jess climbed a wheel and shook Gil Applegate. The old driver grunted and raised his head. A gun was in his hand.

"Get up," Jess said.

Applegate groused. "This is a helluva early start."

"The horses are gone. Along with Donovan, Dallas, and fourteen others."

Applegate's toothless jaws sagged as Jess swung down. Then he began to mouth curses as he produced a pair of plates and jammed them into his mouth.

They wore out the night in vigilance. Susan Shelby awoke when the smoke of the breakfast fire drifted across the coach where she was sleeping. There were sounds of her dressing, and at last she appeared and came toward the fire in the brisk early morning. She stopped in surprise, and gazed about. There was no sign of saddle horses, and there was a grim handful of men squatting about the fire, eating fried fat pork and thick slabs of bread.

No one looked at her. She got a cup and poured herself coffee. Then she stood by Jess. "There's something wrong," she said. "What is it, Jess?"

"Nothing much. They've moved out, is all. We've still got all the coaches, but they've got the horses."

She gasped and glanced westward at the spot where the horses had been pastured.

Jess smiled. "A hitch? Were they supposed to take you with them?"

She looked at him in quick vexation but she held her anger. "No. Only . . . I don't see . . ."

"What they can do with the horses, if they don't have the coaches? Let's put it another way. What can we do with twelve Concords if we don't have horses to pull them?"

Breckwalter, the ponderous, frowning partner of murdered Sam Ashley, glowered into his tin cup. "Put rock foundations under them and start sod-busting," he said. "I tell you one thing. I ain't going to pull any stagecoach to Mexico City."

Susan sat down. "You mean we're . . . ?"

"Stranded is a good word," Jess remarked. "They took the precaution of packing out most of the food they could carry. Or probably what they did was to drop a sack of meal there and a flitch of bacon there, as we came along the last day. So we can't start hiking back to El Paso, a hundred and seventy miles, without grub. And we can't stay here. We'll have to hike for El Venado, the nearest village, and live on tortillas until we can get back to the States." He started a cigarette. "Patriotism in action is a pretty thing. Patriotism to the Confederate States of Hugh Donovan."

Applegate had been mulling it over painstakingly half the night and still did not comprehend the strategy. "Why didn't they knock us off and take both, right then?"

"Because he was only sure of those fifteen, and we'd have been sure to knock off a few of them if he cut loose on us. But there was this other way that they could get the whole kit without firing a shot. They're holding the horses somewhere, and I've got a notion they're watching us right now. When we start hiking for El Venado, they'll come back *pronto* and hitch up. They'll by-pass El Venado and head for Texas."

Susan put the coffee pot down. "Jess, am I responsible for this?"

His eyes were calm and heatless. "Not necessarily. Not unless you got the map on his orders and let him see it. If you didn't, we'd have to assume he knew the trails anyway."

She stood up, looking at him in bewilderment. "I didn't know! I argued with him when he told me you were a Union agent. He said he'd prove it to me if I'd get the maps. I did, and he pointed out some marks I didn't understand, and copied the part of the trail to Laredo. Jess . . . all of you . . . I'm sorry. He made a fool of me, and I put you into his hands. I'll do anything you tell me to try to make it up."

She waited, and still no one spoke, until Applegate slung his coffee into the fire and growled: "That's a hell of a pot of coffee somebody made. You'd better float a rag in 'er next time."

They puttered about, getting the feel of catastrophe. A couple of drivers commenced walloping dust off the varnished red panels of their coaches with long rags. Applegate removed a wheel and slipped the wheel to the outside of the spindle to dope it with grease. At the fire, Jess was molding ball lead when he saw this. An idea entered his head, nebulous as steam. But he examined it from all angles, buttressed it with conjectures, and it began to acquire shape and force.

Jess walked over and looked at the wheel nut. It was large, hexagonal, slotted for a cotter key. He said — "I'm going to borrow this." — and walked around the coach. He compared it with nuts on the reach-and-bolster assembly, with the nut on the kingpin fastening the tongue to the hound. Carefully he went over the entire stage, but there was not another nut with which the wheel nut could be interchanged. Jess walked back. The driver had slipped the wheel to the inside of the spindle, and was waiting for the wheel nut.

Jess was beginning to smile. "Take a water bucket," he said, "and start taking all the wheel nuts off. I'll help you."

Applegate peered at him, not sure whether he liked the idea. He was one who held that a Concord stagecoach was not far from being divine, and it was sacrilegious to tamper with it. Then he seemed to perceive Jess's idea, and he chuckled and grabbed a wrench.

They went down the line of coaches, removing wheel nuts and adding them to the greasy assortment in the bucket. They performed the same operation on the wagons. Then Jess summoned the other men.

"One of you dig a hole," he said. "We're going to hold a burying. Those coaches won't go far without wheel nuts, and there isn't another nut in the train that will take their place. We're going to bury them here and build a fire over the spot."

He retained the rest of the story until the bucket had been wrapped in a tarp and buried three feet deep. A fire was built on the spot. Jess occupied himself with making up a portable camp kit from the remaining supplies. They were going on a short trip, but it had to look like a long one. He gathered them at the fire once more.

"I'm taking for granted that Donovan doesn't like being out there in the hills on short rations and not knowing much about the Indians. I think he's watching us right now and waiting for us to leave before he comes back to claim the booty. Well, we're leaving. We're going to walk till dark, or until we spot them. Then we're coming back. They ought to make about a hundred yards before they break down. They'll go straight up, but when they come down, they'll begin swapping nuts and bolts around trying to rig up something that will get them through. If it's night, they'll need light to work by. If it isn't, we still have the grass for cover. It's two to one, but we've got to chance it. Anybody got a better idea?"

Susan, standing back a few paces, said: "Yes. I'll stay here and get them away from the stagecoaches while you come in."

They turned to stare at her. She came forward, sober and defiant. Jess tucked his hands under his belt. "Aren't you afraid Donovan will talk you into telling where the wheel nuts are?"

"That's just what I will tell him." She turned and pointed. "I'll tell them they're right up there on the hillside, about two hundred yards away. That will give you a chance to work back."

Dr. Bible pursed his lips. "If I could just open up your head, young woman, and see what's behind this. It's a twenty-four carat idea, Clyman. The only weakness of your plan is trying to get back in without being seen, because without the surprise element we're gone goslings."

"And nobody," Jess speculated, "could do it but Sue. She's the only one they wouldn't shoot on sight. All right," he said, "dig up the bucket and we'll take it with us."

It was the hardest slap he could give her; she did not wince. "You don't have to, but I can understand that you'd feel safer."

Gil Applegate brought a shovel but hesitated before commencing to scatter the embers of the fire. "Or you can kill two mallards with one charge," he told Jess. "You can find out by leaving it here whether she's really had a change of heart. Assuming it makes any damn' difference to you."

They were all looking at him, all but the girl, who had gone back to the coach. In his heart, Jess put it on the scales: Applegate knew damned well it made a difference. It was the only way he could ever be sure of her, but it meant jeopardizing the whole operation to make the test. He shrugged.

"You boys take a vote. I'm ready to leave any time you are."

He walked over and shouldered the canvas roll he had made up for himself. Then he heard someone drop the shovel, and the men went to secure their own bedrolls and their rifles. Jess walked to where Susan stood by the coach, her hand on the door. For a moment he stood before her. She bit her lip, but the tears crowded through. It could be the old strength-through-weakness gambit, Jess supposed, but it didn't seem to matter. He dropped the roll and caught her against him. She began to sob, her face buried against his shoulder, and Jess held her tightly. It went beyond politics, treachery, or anything else, this feeling that bound him to her, and now he knew she was as helpless to fight it as he.

"I've been an empty-headed little fool," she whispered. "Trying to be a gentlewoman, instead of the kind of woman you needed. Why didn't you straighten me out a long time ago?"

Jess's fingers were in her hair; he felt the softness of her bosom against him. "You were the kind of woman I needed right from the first, Sue. How am I going to leave you here?"

"It's the only way," she said. "I'll tell them I refused to go with you. Let's think about Mexico City and, after that, California . . . We'll work something out of this."

Jess was thinking of those things — but Applegate, the doctor, and the rest were already tramping out a patch to the spot on the hillside where the wheel nuts were supposed to be buried. Under his belt he had shoved the revolver he had taken from Ashley's body.

He made her take it. "You won't need this, but it will make you feel better."

"I'll need you though, Jess. Always!"

CHAPTER
SEVEN

They set out in late afternoon in a brief file down the freight road. It sloped gently for a mile, and then climbed a ridge and dipped again. On their right were the mountains. Eastward was a ghost of a peak. They made slow marching, not anxious to get far from the train. The coaches were out of sight in a half hour, but they left Applegate in a nest of boulders on the first ridge, from which he could observe anyone approaching and give the signal.

Before long they stopped to rest. They had made about three miles. Gil had given no signal. He was to come down the ridge if he saw anything and signal with a rag tied to his rifle barrel. The sun was close to the ragged skyline of the Sierra Lagartijas. Warmth was leaving the air. The long shadow of the mountains came across them and a cold breeze flowed down from the north. They marched again.

Jess began to realize how high a tower he had built on a foundation of speculation. Hugh Donovan might play it safe and remain out of reach for a week. The only argument against that was that he would be anxious to get out of the country without delay.

258

The swift desert night flowed over them. They camped and made a fire. But none of them ceased to watch the now lost ridge on their back trail. The night signal would be a charge of powder burned on the ground. They boiled coffee, but no one had a hunger bigger than hard tack could satisfy. They were sitting there, sopping hard tack in coffee, when suddenly all of them lunged to their feet and someone said: "By God, boys!"

The powder had flared too brightly and so briefly that it was difficult to believe it had happened at all. Donovan was coming back.

They left everything by the fire except their rifles. They set out at a jog and rested in twenty minutes. Did the signal mean Donovan was already there or merely on the way? They had to assume it meant he was very close. The road tilted again. They were on the long swale of the ridge. They stopped and blew, and not far off they could hear someone moving carefully among the rocks. They were closer than they had thought.

Jess eared back the hammer of his carbine, in case it was not Gil up there, and walked onto the crest of the ridge. The driver slipped out of the boulders, gripped Jess's arm, and pointed.

"Horses are yonder," he whispered. "They only got here about ten minutes ago. Come down from the foothills."

As he spoke, a lantern wick made a small eye of light among the stages, growing until it was a golden puddle on the trampled earth near the dead fires. Men moved about confusedly. Harness rattled, chains clinked. Then

259

the lantern moved from the camp in quick, swinging arcs. Several men were moving up the hillside.

Jess started down the hill. The plan was for Applegate to take four men and work around to the left, to a point near the cache. They could ambush several men here, if they were lucky. Jess would take on the ones at the camp. The grass, deep and thick, muffled their boot sounds; not far off, on their right, the horses moved restlessly under guard. They walked slowly toward the dark ring of coaches. Applegate led off with his men, making a wide swing to the left. Jess signaled the others down. They began a slow crawl toward the coaches, fanning out to enclose half of it.

They were like this when the shot exploded. One of the horse holders fired blindly into the loose pack of them and shouted.

"Injuns, by God!"

The shot screamed away over the prairie. Jess could see the man limned against the horses. He aimed and fired; the gun kicked like a mule, and the man pitched forward. It was ninety percent luck, but it was one man less to handle, nevertheless. He ran for the coaches and sprawled under the closest one.

Donovan was bringing his men back down the trail, bawling caution. "Spread out! Git clear of them coaches!" But he himself was sprinting back into the arms of danger. He had three men with him, revealed by the lantern. Suddenly he realized he was still carrying it and gave it a sling into the grass. It struck a boulder and shattered; whale oil spread over the rock and immediately was a nightmarish illumination for the scene.

Gil Applegate's guns were hammering. Two of the men with Hugh Donovan staggered. Donovan darted into the ring of coaches. "Out this side!" he bawled.

Jess hadn't a clear shot at him, but he found big Ben Dallas and put the man's shoulders on his sights and squeezed the trigger. Dallas went to his knees, sagged forward on all fours, his head hanging. Behind Donovan, Applegate's heavy artillery was whanging again. It drove the stage man into the trap he had tried to bull the others out of. He sprawled in the litter of camp gear and tried to pick out a target.

Two men who had been trying to repair the tampered wheels dropped their guns and raised their hands. Donovan fired a shot into one of these men and shouted: "Damned chicken-livered sons! They ain't taking pris'ners tonight! Kill or git killed!"

He had emptied his carbine and lay over on his side to pull his Colt. It came out, and his eyes found Jess at last, ambuscaded behind a wheel. He fired two shots so swiftly that the rush of flame and the balls thudding into spokes shook Jess. But he steadied down and got a bead on the gunman.

Donovan pulled himself up as if to rise, stared at Jess a moment, and quietly lay forward across his rifle. The rest of the men were shocked out of any semblance of defense. One of them tried to run, and fell. The rest stood congealed with terror.

Jess said: "Hold your fire, boys. I still need a few drivers. They'll drive hog-tied and unarmed, and I'll dump them in the first *jusgado* I come to. If you'd like that better than frying in hell tonight . . . ?"

They rolled toward Chihuahua City in the morning, sixteen men and a girl. Some of the men rode with irons on their ankles. They would be replaced by Mexican drivers at El Venado, and that, thought Jess Clyman, might not be a bad idea in this country.

ABOUT THE AUTHOR

Frank Bonham in a career that spanned five decades achieved excellence as a noted author of young adult fiction, detective and mystery fiction, as well as making significant contributions to Western fiction. By 1941 his fiction was already headlining Street and Smith's *Western Story* and by the end of the decade his Western novels were being serialized in *The Saturday Evening Post*. His first Western, LOST STAGE VALLEY (1948), was purchased as the basis for the motion picture, STAGE TO TUCSON (Columbia, 1951) with Rod Cameron as Grif Holbrook and Sally Eilers as Annie Benson. "I have tried to avoid," Bonham once confessed, "the conventional cowboy story, but I think it was probably a mistake. That is like trying to avoid crime in writing a mystery book. I just happened to be more interested in stagecoaching, mining, railroading . . ." Yet, notwithstanding, it is precisely the interesting — and by comparison with the majority of Western novels — exotic backgrounds of Bonham's novels that give them an added dimension. He was highly knowledgeable in the technical aspects of transportation and communication in the 19th-Century

American West. In introducing these backgrounds into his narratives, especially when combined with his firm grasp of idiomatic Spanish spoken by many of his Mexican characters, his stories and novels are elevated to a higher plane in which the historical sense of the period is always very much in the forefront. This historical aspect of his Western fiction early drew accolades from reviewers so that on one occasion the *Long Beach Press Telegram* predicted that "when the time comes to find an author who can best fill the gap in Western fiction left by Ernest Haycox, it may be that Frank Bonham will serve well." Among his best Western novels are SNAKETRACK, NIGHT RAID, THE FEUD AT SPANISH FORD, and LAST STAGE WEST. THE PHANTOM BANDIT will be his next **Five Star Western.**